THE FINAL SHOOTOUT

Few knew that the notorious outlaw Sabre Wilde was, in fact, none other than Major Horatio Wilde who had robbed a train of Treasury gold and private government papers. He was now a lawful assassin, working directly for the president, with a mission to seek out and execute all traitors. But Wilde, who feared the consequences of returning the Treasury gold, kept both it and the private papers as insurance. Now he was wanted — dead or alive.

JAMES O. LOWES

THE FINAL SHOOTOUT

Complete and Unabridged

LINFORD
Leicester

First published in Great Britain in 2002 by
Robert Hale Limited
London

First Linford Edition
published 2003
by arrangement with
Robert Hale Limited
London

British Library CIP Data

Lowes, James O.
  The final shootout.—Large print ed.—
  Linford western library
  1. Western stories
  2. Large type books
  I. Title
  823.9'14 [F]

  ISBN 1–8439–5030–8

Published by
F. A. Thorpe (Publishing)
Anstey, Leicestershire

Set by Words & Graphics Ltd.
Anstey, Leicestershire
Printed and bound in Great Britain by
T. J. International Ltd., Padstow, Cornwall

This book is printed on acid-free paper

1

It was siesta time and the man sat rocking drowsily in his chair on the veranda of the Lazy Horse saloon, chewing on a straw, was enjoying the peace and quiet of the town called Robbers' Roost. This was the time of day when the long straggly street was quiet when those who would be drinking in the saloon later on had other things on their mind. It was time to attend to the womenfolk.

Suddenly the rocking ceased as Ron Davies sat up with a jerk, spitting out his straw and narrowing his eyes as he watched the five riders trotting slowly and warily into town.

The bastards! He recognized the gang-leader, that accursed Sabre Wilde, the man with the puckered red scar from a sabre-wound, barely concealed by a bushy black beard. If that wasn't enough confirmation, he saw the she-devil Mexican woman riding beside him and the younger feller who was Wilde's sidekick and behind them came the giant black man and the inscrutable renegade Apache. His guts crawled.

They were still some way from the saloon. They all had that tense awareness about them, ready for instant action.

He'd told the boss he'd made a mistake when they'd come riding in looking for Gideon Lockhart and he'd set them up to be bushwhacked. It looked as if Lockhart had failed and they were back seeking revenge.

Quietly he slid from his chair. He'd better go and warn the boss . . .

Inside the saloon the light was dim compared to the outside glare, but he knew that Jake Gleason would be at the poker-table in his favourite seat, back against the wall and facing the batwing doors. There would be four of them playing cards, and the barman. Sabre Wilde had chosen the most vulnerable

2

time to ride into town. They all looked up as he burst through the door.

'What in hell . . . ' began Jake Gleason. His hands fell away from his gun when he saw that the intruder was Ron Davies.

'Wilde's comin' in with his gang!' Ron's voice was a squeak. Jake Gleason viewed him with contempt. 'I told you it was a mistake to send them into Blackwater Canyon! Goddammit, boss, they look as if they mean business!'

Gleason drew on his cigar, and then, blowing smoke, reached for his whiskey glass.

'Keep your hair on, Ron. There's no proof we deliberately sent them into a trap, but to be on the safe side, Buck, you get yourself out the back and climb on the roof and if you hear gunshots, you let whoever's left outside have it, and don't miss!'

Buck Winter nodded and then looked at Gleason.

'What if it's the woman? She's some looker!'

'Her too. We got plenty of women, so don't go soft.'

Jake Gleason nodded at the barman, who was looking uneasy.

'Right, Nobby, get out the shotgun.'

Nobby reached below the counter and produced the loaded shotgun, put it on the bar top and covered it with a dirty towel.

Jake looked at Ron and his two buddies.

'Are you ready for them? The first sign, boys and we fire first and ask questions afterwards, as usual.'

There were three nods and Ron Davies licked his lips. Christ, he wanted the shit-house. What a situation to be in! No back-up from the usual drinkers, no nothing. He looked to the boss for a sign, but Jake Gleason just sat staring at the double doors waiting.

Then the batwings flew open and Sabre Wilde was standing there, a powerful Peacemaker raking the room.

'The first to move, I'll drill, so don't take any deep breaths,' he rasped. Close

4

behind were George Lucas and Carla, who quickly fanned out. Ron Davies sat with sick realization that the woman was actually enjoying herself and that the gun she held as firm as a rock was aimed at his belly. Vaguely he wondered where the black man was, and the Apache. He held his breath, too frightened to stir.

Jake Gleason managed a smile of welcome which fooled no one.

'Ah, so you've come back! Did you find Gideon Lockhart? He's a very unpredictable feller. If he wasn't up in the mountains, maybe he and his men have other business on their minds. He isn't always where we think he is . . . ' He was babbling but Sabre Wilde's stony stare silenced him. He licked suddenly dry lips and cast his eyes around the near-empty saloon. He wished to God he'd never made the rule to have the saloon to himself during siesta time. It was a mistake. He took a deep breath.

'Look, whatever happened out there

was none of my doing! Lockhart is not one of us! Whatever he does he does on his own.'

'Not from what I heard from one of his men!' Wilde ground out. 'It didn't take the Apache long to make him sing!'

'What . . . what have you come back for?'

'To finish the job we started, is all.'

'What job?'

'We wanted Lockhart and all those who helped to make him what he was, an arms-dealer, a slavetrader and a traitor to his country.'

'We know nothing about him,' Jake Gleason protested sharply. 'Whatever you heard is lies! Anyhow, why should you care? You're an outlaw. We've even got a poster about you and your gang. You're wanted dead or alive and worth a thousand dollars to the man who takes you in! We got the poster on one of our raids.'

Sabre Wilde laughed. It sounded menacing to the men who heard it.

'Why we want him is none of your business. We know of your connections with him. We also know that you set us up.'

'That's a lie!'

'Is it? Then Gideon Lockhart died with a lie on his lips!'

'Lockhart dead?'

'Yes, strung up all neat and tidy-like. He's swinging up there from the highest tree we could find, right outside his hideaway as a warning for anyone going there.'

'So why have you come back?'

'As I said before, to finish the job.'

Jake Gleason's head wagged from side to side as he looked at all three of the outlaws.

'You're joking, aren't you? Listen. I can put you on to a gold stash. You can have it all . . .

Sabre Wilde's gun clicked as the hammer went back.

'I want you all outside. Carla, step over here and keep your eye on the little feller. Come on.' His gun fanned out.

'Unless you want it right here. It would be a right shame to mess up this wood floor.'

Suddenly the barman fumbled with the towel. The shotgun came up just as George Lucas took him in the throat. The shotgun blasted off, the pellets hitting the ceiling as the barman slumped to the ground.

Ron Davies started to snivel. He dropped to his knees.

'For God's sake, I had nothing to do with anything! I've got a wife and two kids! I don't want to die!'

'Nobody wants to die, mister, but sometimes the time comes mighty quick. Now all of you run! We'll give you a chance which is more than you would have given us!' Sabre laughed and shot at the feet of Jake Gleason. Gleason turned to run. Sabre put up his hands to stay Lucas and Carla, who were ready to fire.

'Wait a minute, guys. Let them hope they might escape and fire when I say.'

Just then a couple of bullets came

screaming down as Buck Winter aimed at the group. But his aim was spoiled by a lithe figure that came round an adobe chimney and caught his arm. Buck found himself staring into the copper-coloured face of an Apache Indian. His eyes bulged as Johnny Eagle Eye's knife plunged into his heart. Then his body was rolling off the roof and Johnny was leaping down onto a water-butt and onto the ground where he joined Sabre and the gang.

Then Sabre's arm came down in military fashion.

'Fire!' As the astonished townsfolk came out to see what all the row was about they saw the boss of the town and his buddies fall in a ragged line.

They watched in silence as the strangers forked their horses and prepared to move out, many eyes watching Carla with lust in their eyes. She was like a cat sitting astride her black horse, her eyes flashing and her smile feline.

As they moved away, Sabre Wilde saw

the poster tacked on the saloon wall. He saw the headline DEAD OR ALIVE and the pencilled sketch of him showing his cicatrix. He snatched it up and shoved it into his vest pocket. Then they were galloping out of the town known as Robbers' Roost. Their mission was over.

⋆　⋆　⋆

General Fothergill read the brief telegraph message with satisfaction. So the infamous Gideon Lockhart and his close associates had got what they deserved. He had to give the major credit. He always succeeded, no matter how complicated the orders were. The President should be proud of him. He couldn't wait to report to the White House and tell the President that one of the most dangerous traitors of the Civil War had been rounded up and executed. It was a pity that Wilde and his men couldn't get public acclaim for what they were doing.

General Fothergill knew of the growing reputation of the outlaw, Sabre Wilde. It could be that Wilde and his men were enjoying what they were doing. It made him uneasy sometimes. As the years passed, were they becoming more inhuman? These thoughts had come to him many times. Where would it all end?

There was no one to talk to about this aspect of the situation. Major Wilde and his captain, George Lucas, were known in the army now as renegades. They couldn't possibly come back and take up their real places in society. How long could all this last and what would be the outcome? He must talk to the President again and persuade him that they must start a new life.

He sighed. Many times he'd broached the subject but President Johnson was adamant. Let Wilde deal with the traitors who helped to keep the war going far longer than it should have done. Even now, three years on, there were traitors to be caught and shot.

11

He called for his carriage and made his way to the White House where he was admitted on sight.

His thoughts were chaotic as he walked up the wide marble stairs leading to the President's office suite. He nodded absent-mindedly to the dark-clad security guards standing at intervals. He had too much on his mind to be pleasant. Some of the guards watched him and frowned. General Fothergill was usually a genial man. Something must be wrong.

The President's secretary greeted him with a smile and waved him to a seat.

'The President is in conference just now. If you care to wait here, I'll order you some coffee.'

The general groaned inwardly. Waiting made it harder. At least it gave him time to collect his thoughts.

'Thank you.' He sat in gloomy silence waiting to be admitted to the Oval Office.

At last a small harassed-looking man

came out of the office. He glanced at the general and nodded.

'You're in for a rough time, General. He's in a helluva temper! I've nearly had my ear ripped off!'

General Fothergill gave a weak grin.

'Nothing new in that, Berny. I'm used to his sudden explosions and I'll live! You look in need of a stiff drink!'

'Sure and that's what I'm going to get right now!' The general watched the Minister of Internal Financial Affairs scurry away, presumably to the bar and rest-room on the floor below.

The secretary went into the office and returned looking a bit flushed a minute later.

'He's ready for you now, sir, but watch yourself.' He finished in a near whisper. General Fothergill braced himself. It was like being under fire from the enemy.

'Good morning, Mr President, sir.'

'What's good about it, Fothergill? Well? I expect you've brought me some good news. I could do with some! That

13

little creep is rattling his drum about the deficit in army funds again. By God, that major of yours has caused a hell of a lot of trouble. If it gets out that we practically handed the bastard that gold from the Treasury on a plate, God knows what the Republicans will make of it. Well? What have you got for me?'

General Fothergill laid the file on the wide oak desk. The President groped for his spectacles, looked at the top page, then looked over them to the general.

'You don't expect me to wade through this lot, do you? Give me it straight, dammit!' General Fothergill gulped.

'Major Wilde and his men have located and . . . er . . . disposed of the targets named on this list.' He pointed out a page of neatly printed names. 'These have all been eliminated during the past nine months, sir. They have done very well indeed, much better than I expected, the latest being Gideon Lockhart.'

'Lockhart, hey?' The President drummed his fingers on the desk and looked at the general. 'Sit down, for Chrissake! What in hell's the matter with you? Tell me about Lockhart.'

The general sighed. It was going to be a long haul.

'They could only locate him after they'd staged a train robbery. It was in his territory and he came after them. It's all in the deposition, sir if you will read it.'

'Mm-mm, maybe I will at that. Talking of robberies, isn't he going a bit too far? Washington's bouncing with rumours about the feller and his men. He seems to be enjoying the role of outlaw. What in hell's going on?'

'Look, sir, he's got to have a reputation. He can't just renege on the army and then disappear. He took that gold off that train, which we arranged, so that he could move freely around the country. The orders were that all targets were to be executed . . . '

'Bushwhacked is the word for it,

Fothergill, in the West!'

'Er . . . yes. I prefer executed as being a more military term, sir.'

'Executed, bushwhacked or murdered, it doesn't matter a damn. It's punishing all those who betrayed the Government when we were at war that counts.'

'Major Wilde and his trusted men have done a good job. It's a pity we cannot make their exploits public, sir.'

'Hell! That's the last thing we want! We want no public scandals. As it is, the Republicans are wanting a change of government and they're beginning to kick up! Now what I want to know is, what are you doing to get that gold back into the government coffers?'

So the question that General Fothergill dreaded was being asked. This would start the fireworks off with a vengeance!

'Sir, at my last meeting with the major I did indeed indicate that the gold should be returned forthwith.'

'Did he give an explanation of why we are still waiting to receive it? The arrangement was that after that first raid on the army train, orchestrated by you, the bullion would be secretly returned to the Treasury. Why the long delay?'

'Sir, Major Wilde does not intend to return it, not now or ever. He reckons it is an insurance for himself and his men if times change and a new government comes into being!'

For a moment there was dead silence. Then the President roared, throwing his inkpot across the room.

'Like hell he is! Who the hell does he think he is? He's a jumped-up ex-major, given orders to do a certain job for his country. He has no right to make any decisions about that gold! The sonofabitch should be shot!' Johnson banged his desk with his fist. 'I want that gold back in Washington before I leave office! Jesus Almighty! A goddamn army officer fingering his nose at me! I won't have it! You hear me? I'll have him court-martialled!'

'You can't, sir, he's not in the army

17

now, not publicly, that is,' the general said quietly.

'You mean to tell me he can get away with it?'

'Sir, he was a good officer and loyal. We made him what he is today.'

'Dammit, Fothergill, you sound as if you condone what he is doing!'

'Sir, I think we should be careful and think about this. He did say there was a strongbox on that train, and in it some very confidential papers which the Republicans could make trouble with if they came to light.'

The President stared at him, his neck stuck out like a scrawny crow's.

'You mean . . . ?'

'Yes, some of those private dealings we had during the war. You remember, the arrangements with the arms factory and the arsenal and . . . '

'Yes, yes, you needn't go on. I remember.' Suddenly the fire had left the President. He sat quietly staring into space, his long bony fingers drumming on the desk. The sound was driving Fothergill mad. What hellish notion was the President concocting now?

At last Johnson leaned back in his chair and gazed at the ceiling. It was as if he didn't want to lock on to Fothergill's eyes.

'There's only one thing for it, General, and it's a military matter. The outlaw known as Sabre Wilde must be hunted down and er . . . executed. I think that was the word you used?'

'But, sir . . . '

'You heard me, General, that's an order!'

'But we'll never get the bullion back if he's killed!'

'He's too dangerous to live. We've got to get those papers back too. They will be wherever the gold is hidden.'

'But how . . . ?'

'Easy enough. We hunt the men with him. We target the young one. I think if I remember correctly he was a private. There was also a sergeant. We find them both and persuade them to talk.

They would know where the bullion's stashed. It stands to reason that if Wilde was killed they would know the location of the gold.'

'But the major was only carrying out orders!'

'He didn't carry them out far enough. That gold should have been returned to the Treasury.'

'But you can't blame him for what he did, sir!'

The President frowned, his eyes piercing as he looked at the general, who was sweating.

'I'm beginning to think you have some private arrangement with the major, General. Are you sure you don't know where the gold is stashed?'

The general looked shocked. He turned white.

'Mr President, sir! That is a most outrageous statement!'

'Well? Have you?' and the general nearly choked at the steely accusing glance.

Helpless rage engulfed him. How

could the President think this of one of his most loyal military commanders!

'Sir, I have spent a lifetime in the service of my country and have served under ten presidents, whether Democrats or Republicans, and my whole thought was for the honour and glory of this country and I consider it an insult to ask me such a question!'

'You have not answered me, General.'

'You should know the answer, sir! I have never had any private arrangement with Major Wilde and I never will have. Perhaps I should resign my position here at the White House. A younger man would be better suited to your purpose!'

Fothergill glared at the President and stood up, turning to leave the office.

'Hold it, General! I don't want this situation with Wilde to go any further. It is between you and myself. I give the orders and you see they are carried out. Wilde has done a good job. Purged the ranks, as it were. But he's become dangerous and out of hand. I had to ask the question, General. I'm sorry. I should have known better.'

'Sir, isn't there any other way of dealing with Major Wilde?'

'Not unless we capture him and lock him in some dungeon to rot! Better be shot than that.'

Johnson sat chewing his lip for a while and then looked up at Fothergill.

'No, he's got to disappear, killed off as an outlaw. God knows there's enough territory out there for any man to disappear into. See to it, General.'

'But sir . . . '

The President leaned forward pointing a finger. 'Have you forgotten that file of papers? If Hayes got hold of them, the government would collapse and Hayes would walk away with the presidency! Find Wilde and his men and get that damned gold and above all, bring me those papers! That's an order!'

2

Sabre Wilde had been uneasy ever since his meeting with General Fothergill. Now he stared into the fire, oblivious to those about him, thinking over the conversation and recalling the closed look on the old man's face. Dammit! There was something brewing!

He and his followers were holed up in a cave in Washington State, not far from the railway spur where he had met the general.

It was an audacious gamble that paid off, but Sabre never pushed his luck. The cave held only the bare necessities for a one-night stopover. It was barely big enough for both men and horses, but when they rode out at the crack of dawn the cave entrance was concealed and Johnny Eagle Eye brushed the dry dusted ground with a tree branch to obliterate their passing. Sabre could nearly guarantee that no one would come upon the hideaway by chance.

Now he was waiting for dawn to break. Carla and George Lucas were fast asleep and Joshua, the ex-slave, was lying across the opening. Sabre wasn't sure whether the black man was asleep. As usual, Johnny Eagle Eye slept out under the stars.

The uneasiness had caused him a sleepless night. The general's questions abut the gold bothered him. Oh, there had been questions before, but this time they were more insistent. For the first time he'd asked for the location of the cache. Whether it was in Washington State or further west. He'd also wanted to know about Roscoe and Ned Skinner and something had stopped Sabre from telling him just where the two of them had settled. He'd also omitted to tell him about Jodie, the youth whom Roscoe had taken under his wing when Sam Small died.

That had been the first time that he and George had gone back to the cache of gold and taken out Roscoe's and Ned's share of the proceeds. In Sabre's eyes it was fit and proper that government gold should provide the two ex-soldiers with a future. After all, they had earned their freedom. They'd been loyal and acted under orders and the two youths needed to begin a new life.

Sabre frowned worriedly as he watched the wood splinter and spurt amongst the embers of the fire. He reached for the coffee-pot and placed it amongst the glowing embers. Maybe a hot cup of coffee would dispel this nerve-prickling unease.

But it didn't. He was moody when he ate his cold breakfast along with the others. He looked up as Johnny joined them, a jack-rabbit in his hand. He grinned.

'Something for Carla to cook before we get riding.' He tossed it to her, squatted by the fire and reached for the coffee.

'No time for that,' snapped Sabre.

'We leave in ten minutes!'

They all looked at him with concern.

'Why the hurry?' George Lucas asked carefully. There was always a reason when Sabre took that tone of voice.

'I just want to get as far away from here as possible. I have this feeling . . . ' He shrugged. 'Guess I've a goose walking over my grave, is all.'

Johnny looked at him strangely.

'Not a goose, boss. The spirits are warning you. Always take heed of your instincts. If you say we must get out fast, then we ride!'

He stood up with one swift movement, taking a hunk of bread and a thick slice of cold bacon in his hand. 'I go to find a branch to sweep the ground. I'll be back pronto!'

So it was that the small party was soon galloping west and all signs of activity around the cave were smoothed away. The wind would, in time, blow sand up against the boulder that hid the entrance to the cave.

They were heading back to the

Indian Territory and their hideout in the desertlands.

For the first time, General Fothergill had had no orders for them and this also worried Sabre. It was most unusual. It was as if they were being cut off . . .

Sabre kept all his thoughts to himself. Back in their hideout would be time to discuss the situation with the others. Now was no time to worry them.

They were cautious. They kept clear of the towns. Carla had made sure they all carried enough rations to last a couple of weeks. They could live off the land and tighten their belts if they had to. It was essential that no one could recall their passing if a nosy agent was on their trail.

They followed the railway spur for several days before riding across country. Twice every day they could hear the hooting of the trains until they were so far west that all civilization seemed to have disappeared.

They passed through pastureland with great herds of longhorns grazing, then abruptly they were into scrubland that turned into near desert. But now there was not so much tension in them. They were on their way and there were very few eyes to see their passing.

Suddenly there was change. Far ahead, over the rise of a hill, they could hear gunfire. They slowed their mounts and Sabre motioned for Johnny to go ahead. The ex-scout kicked his horse's ribs and moved off in a smooth gallop.

Soon he was back. Jerking his head back over he said tersely:

'Trouble ahead. Looks like some city feller mixin' it with Big Barny and his boys! He's holed up behind some boulders and he can sure shoot! What do we do, boss? Go in and rough up Big Barny? We owe him one!'

Sabre grinned. A bit of excitement could relieve the tension.

'Yeah, let's take a look-see and see

what it's all about.'

They rode on and drew up at the top of the hill.

Sabre took it all in at a glance, the still bodies in grotesque attitudes, the riderless horses, the dead mules below where the city gent was holed up behind some huge boulders. He was blazing away like he knew what he was about.

'Some shooter, whoever he is,' muttered George Lucas. 'I wonder what he's doing in these parts.'

'We'll soon know.' Sabre Wilde waved his arm in a military charge and they thundered down the hill to the clearing below.

Three figures began to run for their horses. Sabre recognized Big Barny by the distinctive black headgear with the eagle's feather tucked into the crown. He took a snap shot at him but missed and watched him thunder away along a narrow defile followed by the other two men.

George Lucas drew a bead on the last

man, saw him rear in the saddle but he galloped on.

Then they were down in the clearing and walking their horses warily, waiting for the lone gunman to show himself.

'Ho, there,' bawled Sabre, 'we come as friends.' He held up both hands empty of firearms, the others strung out in a line behind him.

A short, broad-shouldered man with the rounded belly of a saloon-keeper, stepped from behind a huge boulder, a pistol in one hand and a Spencer rifle in the other. He dropped the rifle and wiped his sweating face with a handkerchief.

'You all must be friends when you send those sonsabitches off with fleas in their ears! Pity you didn't get the big feller. I was watchin' you and gettin' a breather.'

'You're lucky we happened along, mister. D'you know who was gunnin' for you?'

'Nope, and I don't care! I'm still alive which is more than I can say for this poor bastard.' He bent and grabbed the foot of a body lying behind the rocks.

Sabre and the rest dismounted. Joshua went to help the little man to drag the body clear of the loose rocks.

He glanced down at the body and sucked in his breath. He recognized the face even though part of the head had been blown off. What in hell was this city man doing with Ikey Norris?

'Hey, boss, you sure want to see who this is!'

Sabre, studying the little man's grey store-suit, the bowler hat perched on the back of his head and the relative cleanliness of the white linen shirt and coloured tie, stepped up to and crouched over the body. He too drew a sharp breath.

'Ikey Norris! How come you're travelling with him?'

The little man shrugged. 'We got together in Carson's Creek. I had merchandise to trade and he was acting agent for his boss . . . '

'Who is Max Berenger, one of the

31

most powerful outlaws in these and any other parts. He's a long way from home.'

The little man's eyes widened and his right hand instinctively groped for his pistol. Joshua, who was nearest to him moved closer, his heavy Peacemaker digging into the fat man's back.

'I wouldn't if I were you,' he said into his ear.

The little man looked alarmed.

'Look, fellers, it's not what it seems. I'm merely on the way to meet a client and this feller was sent to take me to him. As far as I know, this Max Berenger is a genuine first-class buyer.'

'And what are you totin', mister?'

'That's none of your business! I'm grateful for your timely intervention, but I'd like to ride on after this here feller is buried!'

'But you say you're a stranger around these parts. How will you find Max Berenger?'

The man shrugged. 'I can ask at the next town, I guess.'

'Which by my reckoning is about two hundred miles away. You could be crow-meat before another day's out.'

Suddenly George Lucas stepped forward. He yanked the man's jacket down over his arms so that his arms were pinioned and felt through his vest pockets. He came up with a wad of papers. Silently he handed them over to Sabre.

'Have a look at those, boss. I never knew a city gent move without a thick file of papers on him. They'll tell us who he really is!'

The little man scowled.

'I'm Dan Tompkins and I work for the Lucas Small Arms factory and I've the authorization to prove it!'

He did not see the looks Sabre Wilde and George Lucas exchanged.

'How long have you worked for them?' George Lucas asked sharply.

'Oh, nigh on twenty years. I'm one of their most successful agents. Me and old Lucas are like that!' He put up two fingers close together.'

'You're a lying son of a bitch!' George Lucas spat out. 'I know all the Lucas agents and you're not one of them!'

The man glanced around furtively, his eyes like a frightened rabbit's. He saw them all closing in on him, and the menace erupting from the ex-scout who was running a finger along the blade of his knife was turning his bowels to water. Even the woman reminded him of a cat sharpening her claws, her slanted eyes gleaming in anticipation . . . of what? He licked his dry lips.

'Listen, fellers, I've got a cache of rifles, some small arms and some ammunition. I'll admit I was goin' to trade with Max Berenger, but you can have the lot at a cut-price rate. What about it?'

'Is that why Big Barny was after you? He knew who you were?'

'Yes. I'd done a deal with him and this here feller came along and offered more, so I ditched that son of a bitch and he come after us! That's the story. I swear on my mother's grave!'

'Mmm, what shall we do with him, fellers?'

Carla slid forward.

'Leave him to me, Sabre.' She grinned. 'I'll give him the Mexican version of the Spanish Inquisition!'

'You keep out of this, Carla. This is men's business!' She moved away sulkily, her beautiful face ugly in her disappointment.

Johnny Eagle Eye moved, looking around with that inscrutable air that missed nothing.

'I go and take a look-see and check that Big Barny is not returning with reinforcements,' he said. Without waiting for Sabre's say-so, he rode away.

Joshua waited. He would do whatever the boss commanded. To Joshua, this little man was only white trash, the kind who'd given him hell when he was a slave, like a puffed-up pigeon with back-up, but shit-scared on his own. Joshua had a great contempt for such men.

'Tie him up, Joshua, and we'll eat while I go through these papers. Carla, get the grub out. We'll eat cold. No need to light a fire and let the whole world know we're here.'

So while the meal was laid out by Carla, Sabre and George Lucas examined the papers found on Dan Tompkins. It soon became clear that he was a gun-runner and dogsbody for a man in Washington by the name of Marcus Shane who worked in the Treasury Department.

Marcus Shane! Sabre tapped the papers. Where had he heard that name before and in what connection? It worried him. It was strange that someone from the Treasury should pop up in the same vicinity as themselves, especially in the circumstances when the Treasury was taking such an interest in the gold that was buried.

It niggled Sabre Wilde. It would be better to have Dan Tompkins with them. He also wanted to know about Marcus Shane's activities. It would be something to report to General Fothergill.

Johnny returned. All was clear. There was no sign of Big Barny for the moment, but Sabre knew that they had not heard or seen the last of him.

The scratch meal ready, Sabre looked down at the trussed-up Tompkins.

'Can we trust you if the ropes come off so's you can eat?'

Tompkins gave an ingratiating grimace that was supposed to be a smile.

'Sure. I've no quarrel with you, mister. I take it you're no friend of Big Barny's. Neither am I, so what's the quarrel between us?'

'You said you were an agent of Lucas Small Arms and we know you're not! You lied. Now why did you do that?'

Dan Tompkins started, his eyes widening.

'How the hell did you know that?'

'None of your business. But why pass yourself off as one of their agents?'

The man shrugged. 'Got to have a cover. You folk are outlaws so it don't signify. I'm a small arms gun-runner and I've got to have a respectable cover-story. It don't matter with you boys.'

For a long moment Sabre studied him while the others waited. Then Sabre nodded to Joshua.

'Loose him, Josh, but watch him!'

Dan Tompkins grinned as the ropes came off, but his eyes remained cold, watchful.

'Thanks, mister and I'm sure hungry!'

They ate, and while they ate, Sabre asked questions about Max Berenger. Either Tompkins was lying or he genuinely didn't know much about the man except that he was a keen buyer.

'Look here, mister. Everyone's heard of Max Berenger. How come you know so little about him?' George Lucas burst out. The little man looked nervously around at them all. He didn't like the grim faces and a cold chill went up his spine. He had to watch his mouth now.

'My boss gave me my orders. I was to

meet up with the guy and find out what he wanted and how much he would pay for quick deliveries. I was to telegraph the result to the boss and wait at the nearest railroad depot and see that the goods were delivered. That's all I know and may I drop dead if I lie!'

Sabre's question came like a flash of lightning.

'Who's your boss?'

Dan Tompkins swallowed, cursing inwardly. He'd done the very thing he'd wanted to avoid.

'I can't tell you that. He'd have me shot.'

'You'll be shot if you don't tell us!' Sabre's gun suddenly dug him in the ribs.

George Lucas froze, his mug of coffee forgotten in his hand. Joshua and Carla stared and waited. They both knew that something important was coming up. Only Johnny Eagle Eye, sitting some distance away, kept on eating, his eyes fixed on the far distant hills.

The sudden silence was broken by Tompkins' yelp as Sabre Wilde's gun dug deep again into the man's side.

'Hey! Steady on there, you'll crack my ribs,' Tompkins howled.

'There'll be more than ribs cracked if you don't answer the question!' They all heard the gun's click as it was cocked.

'Jesus Christ! I'm a dead man if I tell you!'

'You're a dead man if you don't.'

'All right, damn you to hell! It's Marcus Shane!'

'You're lying. Marcus Shane is your contact. Who's his boss?'

'For the love of God — '

'Don't give me that crap! Marcus Shane works for the Treasury, doesn't he?' At Tompkins' nod Sabre went on, 'He's the front man, but front men always have a shadowy boss who can't be fingered. Right?' Again Tompkins nodded. 'So who is he?'

'I tell you I don't know! All I know is that I get orders from Shane and I report to him and the trade goods . . . '

40

'You mean guns and ammunition?'

'Yes. They come by rail to wherever I happen to report from. I make arrangements about payment by telegraph to a bank in Washington and that's all there is. I swear it!'

'How d'you get paid?'

'I take my cut before the funds are telegraphed.'

'In whose name?'

Tompkins swallowed hard as if his throat and tongue were dry.

'Aloysius Dart!' he gasped out.

There was the sound of indrawn breath and Tompkins saw with alarm that the two white outlaws were looking at each other with dismay which was fast turning to anger.

'What's wrong, fellers? I'm telling the truth, I swear it!'

'I believe you,' Sabre Wilde said solemnly. 'I'm goin' to talk to Lucas here. You get busy with a spade. I want those guys buryin' before we leave at dawn tomorrow. Carla and Joshua, you clean up the camp and leave everything

41

shipshape. I want no sharp-eyed scouts cuttin' our trail. I've got an itch I can't scratch but I sure think we should get to hell out of this country and lie low for awhile.'

He nodded to George Lucas and they moved away, both still stunned by the name of Aloysius Dart.

They walked over to the tethered horses and Sabre ran a practised hand down the foreleg of the nearest.

'What you think, Lucas? There's only one man who could come up with that name.'

'Yeah, it's the name you contact Washington with. There's only one man who answers to it.'

'General Fothergill himself! You think Fothergill's playing both ends to the middle, or is he actin' under orders for the big boss himself?'

George Lucas gave him a sharp glance. 'What you're implying is treason. You don't really think the President would . . . ?' He didn't finish what he was about to say.

'He's only a man after all and he's comin' to the end of his term of office.'

'We don't know for sure, boss. It could be old Fothergill who's takin' advantage of the President. He'll be retirin' I should think when Johnson goes. It stands to reason. A Republican could be the next president and he'd be all washed up.'

'You know what that means, Lucas?'

'You mean about us?'

'Yeah. Fothergill was kind of strange when I saw him. I didn't want to worry you needlessly, but I had a screwy feelin' about him. It was about that gold. He was more pressin' than usual about where it was stashed.'

'You didn't tell him?' George Lucas asked sharply.

'What kinda fool you think I am?'

'You think he and the President want to get their hands on it? I have a feelin' it wouldn't go back to the Treasury.'

'That's what I think. I also think we're in for the chop! If they get their hands on that gold they'll want no witnesses to what happened to it. As outlaws, we can be gunned down and no questions asked!'

George Lucas stared at him. 'But you got those papers?'

'Yeah, but they're buried with the gold. If the President's bloodhounds find that gold . . . '

'How could they?'

'Easy, dammit! Send some nosy little agent like that Tompkins down into Texas and anybody there could tell them where our hideout is! It would be just a matter of time!'

'So we go pick up the gold and leave Texas.'

'You think it's that simple? What about Roscoe and Skinner and that kid, Jodie, they took with them? Roscoe and Skinner know the location if not the exact spot.'

'But they've assumed new names and Roscoe's now got two sons.'

'You think that will stop 'em? If the Pinkertons are put on the job, they'll find 'em or bust!'

'So what do we do, boss?'

'Turn south and head for Arkansas and let's hope we get to Roscoe before they do.'

'And what about this feller, Tompkins?'

'Mmm, maybe keep him with us for a while, and give him enough rope to see what he does. The gun-running could be a blind. He could have been on the lookout for us, or at least sniffin' our trail.'

'Come to think of it,' mused George Lucas, 'it was a bit of a coincidence, him popping up like that.'

They turned and studied the little man digging a grave. He was sweating, obviously not used to manual labour. Sabre nodded as if he had come to some decision.

'Yeah, we'll give him enough rope . . .'

It was a very subdued Dan Tompkins who travelled with them. There was always someone watching him. At night he found himself bedding down with a smiling Joshua, but the smile didn't reach his eyes. His bones ached, his leg

45

muscles turned to jelly. He hoped to God Max Berenger was at the meeting-place and ready to buy what he had to offer. It would give these sons of bitches proof of his story and then they might let up on him. He had a lot to report to Aloysius Dart, if only he could get to a telegraph office.

His papers, which the bastards had scrutinized, had told them exactly where the meeting was to take place. He couldn't even lie about it. He wished he'd never been lured into this Aloysius Dart business, but the money offered had been good and it all sounded so easy . . .

They rode into the little town of Beaver Lodge, a straggling street of log cabins, a couple of saloons and a dry-goods store. Carla immediately dismounted outside the store, tethered her mount and, with a laugh at the others, strode inside to replenish her tattered wardrobe. Johnny Eagle Eye elected to watch the horses and the others went into the saloon called Dolly's Place.

Dolly was old and fat, her hair dyed a fiery red which matched the thick lips heavily painted. A coating of lead-based white chalk made her face look like a mask. Sabre reckoned she was trying to hide the ravages of smallpox scars. But her laugh was jolly and her voice boomed as she welcomed them inside.

'What's it to be, boys? The first drink is on the house!' She looked Sabre over, then her eyes travelled to George Lucas, then back to Sabre. 'And I might add that anything else you want can be had at a price!' The huge lips puckered suggestively. The little man and Joshua she ignored completely.

Sabre looked down at her and laughed, showing white teeth. She drew back. He reminded her of a hunting wolf.

'Never mind what else we might want. We'll buy our drinks and be under no obligation.' He threw some coins on the bar counter. Dolly frowned.

'What's it to be then, gents?'

'Beer all round and a bottle of your best whiskey.'

She served them right smartly for such a fat woman. They drank appreciatively.

'So? Have you ridden far?' she asked as they drank.

'You might say so. My friend here is looking for Max Berenger. You know of him?'

Sabre saw the woman's face change.

'What's he want him for?'

'That's his business.' He looked around the saloon and noted the drunk asleep in one corner. The rest of the place was empty.

'You don't get much trade here?'

'Not passing-through trade. We're busy at night.'

'Does Max Berenger come here at night?'

'Nope.'

'You *do* know him, don't you?'

'Yeah, I know the son of a bitch! He uses this place like it was his own. He's that mean he wouldn't give you a bad

48

cold! He killed a man in here once and he left me to pay to have him carted away to Boot Hill and never offered me a dime for my trouble! He's a lowdown sidewinder and I'd like to . . . ' She stopped as the batwing door swung open and a big man stepped inside. Her face changed into a puddingy ingratiating smile.

'Ah, Mr Berenger, sir, welcome! What would you like to drink?'

The little man turned to greet him.

'Max! We've been waiting for you. Is all well?'

Sabre and George Lucas turned leisurely to study the newcomer. He moved easily to the bar, smiling at Dan Tompkins.

'Hya, Dan. Yes, all's well. What have you for me this time and who're your friends?'

He was clean-shaven, his hair a faded blond shading to grey. He had strong shoulders and the gunbelt showing under a leather jerkin held twin .45s. His boots were scuffed but Sabre recognized army issue when he saw it.

He reckoned this man was disciplined and dangerous.

The little man turned to Sabre.

'This is Sabre Wilde and George Lucas. Ikey Norris and I were ambushed by Big Barny. Ikey was killed but Wilde and his bunch came along in good time and saved me.'

'Ikey dead, eh? He was a good feller.' But Berenger didn't show much regret. 'What happened to Big Barny?'

'He got away, Max.'

'A pity. He's a dangerous bastard, Dan. You should have never tangled with him. I warned you!'

The little man shrugged.

'Yeah, I should have listened to you.'

Max Berenger turned to the listening men.

'So, you're Sabre Wilde. I've heard about you.' He stuck out a meaty fist for Sabre to shake.

'I've heard about you, too.'

They both laughed and Max Berenger nodded to Lucas and Joshua, and then said softly, 'I heard you had a woman with you. Mighty convenient!'

Sabre frowned. 'Convenient?'

'Yeah, you know . . . you'll never suffer from woman-starvation, any of you!'

That was when George Lucas stepped forward and his fist connected with Berenger's chin, sending him flying through the air before hitting the dirt floor.

'What in hell . . . ?' began Berenger, fingering his chin.

'That's for insulting the lady,' George Lucas grated, his temper flaring. 'If you want to make more of it, get up and I'll hit you again!'

'Easy, easy,' Sabre muttered. 'Remember why we're here, will ya?' Lucas gave him a filthy look.

'If you aren't upset at what he implied, I am. Carla's not a tramp.'

'Calm down, George. Carla's not here and she'll never know, so watch yourself! That temper of yours can get you into trouble.'

Max Berenger was scrambling to his feet. With his head stuck out he was like a shambling bull.

'Why, you son of a bitch, I'll wipe the floor with you!' He came with a run at George, arms swinging. George deftly swung aside and hit him again as he charged, this time on the side of his face. Berenger fell to his knees. Then, as he scrambled to rise, his right hand went for his gun; as he twisted around Sabre Wilde's foot came down hard on his wrist.

'Easy now, mister. No need for gunplay. You're here to do business with Dan. Who're you workin' for? We know about Aloysius Dart. Who's the big shot?'

Max Berenger lay back rubbing his jaw, eyes sparking venom.

'I don't know and if I did, I wouldn't tell you. It's none of your business.'

'I'm makin' it my business! You're buyin' guns and ammo from this here punk whose contact is Aloysius Dart. Now I know that Dart is a contact in Washington for someone higher up. I want to know who he is! So sing, mister or I'll cripple you up, good!'

'Look, all I know is that I buy army surplus. What I do with it is my business. I pay what's agreed, wait a couple of weeks and collect at a stated railroad station. The arrangement's good. I've never been let down yet, and as for the cash, I couldn't give a shit where it goes or who to. It's his business after I've paid up. Rough him up and leave me alone, will ya?'

'So, who buys the guns from you? Indians and Mexican rebels, I expect.'

Max Berenger glared but did not answer back. There was that certain tension in the air that warned him to take great care. It had been a mistake to mention the woman.

'All right, mister, get up and do your dealin' with Tompkins here and get out.'

'What? With you lot as witnesses! Not likely. This is done in private.'

Sabre Wilde shrugged. 'Then you don't do a deal. That's the end of it.'

Now the hitherto silent Dan Tompkins butted in.

'Say, mister, you have no call to do that. All I need is for him to sign a bit of paper. He gives me the cash and I give him a receipt and a rendezvous to pick up the goods.'

'Then do it.'

The two men approached one of Dolly's empty tables and sat down. The watching men drank Dolly's ale and waited. It was soon done. The two men shook hands and Max Berenger moved off towards the batwing doors.

'I'll be off,' he said over his shoulder. 'The place stinks of pig-shit!' The doors slammed behind him.

Sabre Wilde now regarded Tompkins with narrowed eyes.

'So what comes next, Dan?'

Dan Tompkins looked nervous.

'I take out my cut, make for the nearest telegraph office and send a message to Dart. I wait for his reply and he tells me at which bank to deposit his cash.'

'Then what are we waitin' for? We'll go and find the nearest telegraph office and we'll all wait for his reply!'

3

Sabre Wilde gave Joshua an imperceptible nod. Joshua grinned, knowing what he had to do. He slipped outside the saloon, watched Max Berenger ride out of town, then he gave three sharp whistles. Johnny Eagle Eye, perched high on a hill overlooking the town, saw him wave in the direction of the outgoing rider. At once, Johnny forked his horse and, picking his way down the hillside, went in pursuit. He would follow Max Berenger to his hideaway and catch up the other riders later on. This was what he liked best, to work alone and report back results.

As he rode away he saw George Lucas coming out of the saloon, presumably to look for Carla. He'd watched the Mexican girl go into the store. He grinned. George Lucas was like a hen with one chick where Carla was concerned. Like he'd been with his own squaw, he reflected, until that son of a coyote had lured her away from him when he was away hunting. He rarely thought of that time when the shades of madness had possessed him and he'd slaughtered them both. His face was grim as he followed Max Berenger. Better to be an outcast than laughed at as a cuckold in his tribe.

George Lucas knew where Carla would be. Once inside a town store, she could spend hours looking at the feminine fal-de-lals. Women's clothes were things she sadly missed. George knew how much time society females spent on their wardrobes. He expected Carla to feel the same, especially as she dressed exclusively in men's shirts and pants with a leather jerkin to hide her not very shapely bosom. She looked more like a boy than a girl, especially when she stuffed her hair into one of the hard black Spanish hats which she favoured.

He stepped inside the store and

looked around for the girl. There was only one customer in the women's section and this woman certainly wasn't Carla. She was dressed in a strawberry-pink gown with dark-red velvet bands around the skirt and neck. She had a wasp waist which stirred George when the lady adjusted the wide-brimmed bonnet on her head and peered into a cheval mirror to see the effect of gown and bonnet.

The storekeeper's wife was already parcelling up a number of purchases. George reckoned the lady must be in town from one of the ranches and making the most of her visit.

He coughed. The storekeeper's wife looked at him and smiled.

'Can I help you, sir?'

'We . . . yes . . . I'm looking for a young girl. She's not around. She was wearing a checked shirt and black pants and was wearing a black . . . ' His voice trailed away as the woman in front of the mirror turned sharply at the sound of his voice.

'George! What are you doing in here?'

'Carla? Is that you, Carla?' He swallowed a lump in his throat. 'I didn't recognize you in those duds. You've even got a . . . a . . . ' he stopped. He nearly said bosom. She laughed.

'Go on, say it! Tell the truth and shame the devil! I've got breasts, for God's sake, and they only show because I'm wearing a corset! I've even got a waist!'

George gulped again and now knew why Sabre was adamant that Carla should wear men's gear if she rode with them. Jesus! He'd always fancied her, but in that get-up she was irresistible. It took all his time to remember why'd he'd come looking for her.

'Get out of that gear as fast as you can. We're pulling out, pronto!'

Carla's happy face turned sulky.

'But we've just got here! The son of a bitch's done it on purpose! Surely we could have had one night here?'

'Look, we've got to get to a telegraph

office. Sabre's worried and has got it into his head that trouble's brewing. Now jump to it!' His voice sounded like a crack of a whip.

'There's always trouble brewing. We never have it any other way.'

'Stop acting like a spoiled brat or you'll be left behind. Do you want that?'

'All right. I'll be with you as fast as I can. I take it I can take my new shirt and pants with me? I've also bought some new boots.'

'Yes, but not more than you can carry.'

'What about those extra horses we picked up?'

'They're not pack-animals and we're getting rid of them as soon as possible. We're travelling fast, Carla, and I'm warning you, Sabre will leave you behind if you don't jump to it!'

He knew that was the one thing Carla dreaded, being left behind. Sabre Wilde and the rest of them were the only folk she regarded as family these days since the violent death of her parents. She couldn't bear to be left behind.

George strode out of the store. Carla, apologizing to the staring woman, stripped off and donned her own worn clothes.

'I'm sorry. I really would have liked those things.' She sighed. 'But I'll just pay you for the rest, and go.' Hugging her brown paper parcels to her, she rushed outside to an impatient Sabre, who scowled at her. George and Joshua and the little man, Dan Tompkins were ready to ride. George was holding her horse and she had scarcely time to tie her parcels to her pommel before they were galloping out of town.

They stopped twice to water the horses and eat, Dan Tompkins grumbling about their haste. They hit the railroad and followed it for a couple of hours, finally coming to a railway spur with rails branching south. There they found the telegraph office and saw the telegraph poles marching alongside the tracks.

Inside the office a man of about forty looked up from his desk. He was drinking coffee and studying a railways timetable.

'What can I do for you gents?' he asked.

Dan Tompkins stepped forward nervously.

'I want a message sending to Washington.'

'Right. Want me to send it as you say it, or are you gonna write it down? Can you write?'

Tompkins looked affronted.

'Yes, I can write! Give me one of your forms and then I can calculate how many words to send.'

'Ten words a dollar and after that five cents a word.'

Sabre Wilde and the others stood back and watched while Dan Tompkins laboured over his wordage. When he was finished, he handed it over to the waiting man.

'Just a minute,' Sabre said, swiftly striding forward. 'I sure want to see that message before it's sent!'

The telegrapher looked from one to the other.

'You can't do that, mister. This is a private message and by law I'm not allowed to show you.' He gulped and stared as Sabre drew his gun and held it close to the man's head.

'Don't mess with me, feller. Just hand it over.' He took the form from the man's nerveless hand.

He read the message swiftly and nodded.

'Send it, and we'll wait for a reply.'

Trembling, the man cranked up his machine and the wires began to hum. Soon the dot dot dash of Morse code was sending the message on its way.

Sabre Wilde's face was grim. George, lounging against the door, asked softly,

'What did the message say, Sabre?'

'To Aloysius Dart, Washington. Mission accomplished as arranged. Should ride SW. Please reply rendezvous. Tompkins.'

George Lucas drew a breath. The

message could mean anything, and why say he was riding southwest?

'Why ride south-west, Sabre?'

Sabre shrugged. 'Who says it's south-west?'

'You said . . . '

'I know what I said. The message read SW. It could mean south-west or it could mean Sabre Wilde! Get it!'

George looked at him and nodded.

'The son of a bitch!'

'Just keep quiet and let's see what happens when the answer comes back.'

'Hell, Sabre, are you sure you're not imagining trouble when there is none? After all, you're just going on your inner feelings.'

'Have I ever been wrong when I've had a hunch?'

'Well, no, but you've never questioned the general before.'

'Look, there was something different about him. The son of a bitch couldn't look me in the eye, and there was his insistence on knowing where the gold was stashed.' He took a deep breath.

'There's something brewin', George, I can stake my life on it.'

George Lucas shook his head slowly.

'Well now, if you feel that bad about it, then we'll have to sleep with one eye open.'

'Or not sleep at all!'

'So we just wait and see what message comes back from Aloysius Dart?' It was said a little mockingly. 'Isn't that like waiting like sitting ducks?'

'Look, George, if you don't like it, you know what you can do!'

George Lucas stared hard at the man he'd followed for so long.

'You don't mean that, Sabre?'

'I'm givin' you the chance to pull out. You know where the gold's stashed, you can take your cut and make a new life for yourself. I think I'm the target and it could be rough. I don't want anyone's death on my hands. Is that clear?'

'Jesus! What kind of a bastard d'you think I am? We've been together too long for us to split! We stand or fall together and that goes for Roscoe and young Skinner. Joshua and Carla don't count because they were never involved with hold-ups and Johnny can look after himself. I figure if you're right and there *is* trouble, then we'd better round up Roscoe and those boys mighty fast!'

'That's how I figure it, George. Once we get some inkling of what might be cookin' up in Washington, we'll make for Arkansas and pay those boys a visit. I'd like to see old Roscoe again, anyway.'

'Right. Then the sooner that damn answer comes back for Tompkins the better.'

The hours passed slowly; the burning heat of the sun was hard to bear in the small stuffy office. Carla prowled up and down outside, using her hat to fan herself. Joshua squatted with his hat over his face and snoozed with one ear cocked for any likely diversion.

Inside the office the three men waited while the telegrapher worked at his desk, now and again stopping for coffee. He didn't offer any to the waiting men and they didn't ask for any. Twice the telegraph machine chattered and everyone sat up alert, but it was only a supervisor checking the line.

A train hooted in the distance. Joshua sprang to his feet and watched for its smokestack trundling around a bend, while Carla stood back, half-hidden by the privy. It thundered past without stopping but the driver gave an extra tug on the hooter as he did so.

The sun was casting long shadows when at last the answer to Tompkins' telegraphed message came back. The machine chattered and this time the incoming message was written down letter by letter until it ceased abruptly.

A few scribbles and then the man turned swiftly and with relief handed the message over to Tompkins. Before he could read it, Sabre snatched it from him.

There it was, the confirmation of his

fears. He read the message twice before passing it on to George Lucas. It read, 'Message received. Well done. Will take steps to apprehend SW and tie up loose ends. Will recall other agents. Berenger deal finalized. Payoff as usual. A D.'

George Lucas swore.

'So Marcus Shane is in on it! He's the general's dogsbody, so this little creep here is working for him!'

They both turned on the little man who suddenly got to his feet, a small derringer in his hands.

'Stand back, gents. I only did what I had to do! You don't want me, you want the big men behind all this. I'm getting out and I'll plug the man who tries to stop me!'

Sabre nodded to George.

'Let him go, George. He won't get far.'

Tompkins made a dive for the door, firing a shot into the ceiling as a warning. He slammed outside and made a dash for his horse, but Joshua in a reflex action fired a snap shot. The little man screamed, hit in the thigh, and rolled down amongst the tethered horses, causing them to whinny and kick and rear. Before any of them could drag him clear, he was mashed to a pulp.

Carla watched, her face pale. She wanted to be sick. She'd shot a man before but the sight of a man's face and body being pulverized by maddened horses was something she would never forget.

'Jesus Christ,' muttered George, 'what a way to go! Poor little bastard. If he hadn't panicked he'd be here now.'

'It was his own fault,' Sabre Wilde said harshly. 'Come on, let's be on our way.' Without a further look at the remains, he forked his horse and was ready to ride.

George Lucas frowned. The boss was fast turning into a real killer. He'd seen the gradual change coming over Wilde for quite a while. It was as if he'd stifled his conscience so long that now all vestige of Major Wilde had been subsumed into the personality of the outlaw, Sabre Wilde. He believed that the man he had followed so blindly was now a killer who enjoyed his work.

'What about the corpse?' he asked.

Wilde shrugged. 'What about it?'

'We can't just leave him . . . ' George Lucas began.

'You're too soft, George. You're not a survivor like me. If I wasn't lookin' after you all, you'd be dead within weeks! Now come on, what are you waitin' for?'

George threw some coins to the staring telegrapher, who was standing in his doorway.

'Here, get someone to bury him, mister. Sorry we can't stop.' He rode off after Sabre and the others. He wondered where it all would end.

★　★　★

They all knew there would be a hue and cry when Dan Tompkins' death was reported. It stood to reason that a message to Aloysius Dart would be sent, and those in Washington would be smart enough to know that Wilde and his gang were now alerted to the manhunt which would now be organized.

They turned south. It would be weeks before they eventually reached the place in Arkansas where Roscoe and the boys had taken refuge, if they were lucky and didn't run into any secret agents on the hunt for them.

Sabre Wilde knew that undercover enquiries would be made, and all sheriffs and marshals in all states would be on the lookout for their passing. He should know. In the past he'd used that information himself when they were tracking the President's victims. Now they were the hunters hunted . . .

It meant riding cross-country and avoiding even small hick towns. They would have to live rough off the land. Their supplies were depleted and they couldn't replace what they were short of. They needed Johnny Eagle Eye's expert knowledge at living off the land. Sabre worried about him. It was many days now since he'd gone off after Max Berenger. There was nothing he could do about it, but he continually looked backwards to see if there was any movement behind them. Johnny could follow their trail over hard or soft ground. If nothing had happened to him he would eventually show up, he comforted himself. He kept his worries to himself. No use worrying George or the others. He knew Joshua was troubled, for he and Johnny had been special buddies.

At last he made his mind up to talk to Joshua and get him to backtrail and forage around to look for sign. In the meanwhile they would rest up the horses and do a little hunting themselves. They needed meat badly, any kind of meat, even a rattlesnake would do.

Joshua agreed with him. He was pleased to do something constructive. He'd had his misgivings about Johnny for several days. He wanted action. He was keen to go.

That left Carla and George and himself, so the two men took it in turns to go out hunting and left Carla to rest up and make their scratch meals.

When George's turn came around to hunt Sabre realized he'd made a mistake. Carla wasn't in the mood for resting. She was all out to make trouble for him. It was rare that they should be alone together. Now she came boldly to where he was resting with his back against a tree. At first he wasn't aware of her or her intentions. He was lost in thought, trying to work out a plan of action and what he would do if he were the President. He saw the danger he and his men were in clearly if the President had indeed turned against him for his own ends.

Rumours had abounded over the last few months of the President's coming to the end of his term. If there were dodgy dealings to be dealt with, to leave a clean slate, then there would be others who would have to watch their backs . . .

A shadow fell over his face. He looked up, startled. Carla was standing before him. He smiled.

'Hi! Something I can do for you? You want more wood?' He made to rise. She sank down beside him, shaking her head.

'It's not wood I'm after. Why is it you only think of me as someone to cook and fight? Why don't you see me as a woman?'

She touched his bearded cheek and he pulled away.

'Carla! We've had this argument before, girl. Look, I'm old enough to be your daddy. I'm mighty close to bein' fifty and you're just a kid of twenty. Go on, bring me some coffee and let's forget this, eh?'

'Sabre, I'm a woman and age doesn't matter. I love you, Sabre. You saved my life and I'll do anything you want. You can beat me, torture me but you must love me!' She put her head on to his chest and then said in a more muffled voice, 'I'd kill for you, Sabre, or even die for you. Doesn't that mean something?'

He pushed her away.

'It means you're grateful to me for saving your life. Don't mix that up with being sex-starved, Carla. That's not love, not the kind I know, so get me that coffee!'

She drew back and stared at him, her eyes sparking fire as her temper flared.

'You're a cold bastard, Sabre, or are you frightened to touch me? Have you any feeling under that hard chest of yours?' She swooped to kiss him and she felt his reaction and the quiver that ran through his body. Triumphantly she deepened the kiss, her tongue exploring his mouth. Then he surprised her as his strong arms came about her. He cradled her savagely and she felt the full force of his hard mouth on hers.

Her spirit soared and somewhere inside her something pulsed into life. She wanted him like a mountain cat wants her mate.

Then he was turning her over and she felt his hard hand slapping at her rear. Only the hard canvas of her pants saved her from the brutal assault. She screamed in rage and pain.

'Don't ever accuse me of not darin' to touch you,' he growled. 'I'll make that hot little ass even hotter than it is now if you ever try this stunt again! Now get back to your cookin' and get me that coffee pronto or I'll grab you and drop you in the middle of that creek, by God I will!'

She scrambled away, her backside stinging and hate for him in her heart. She felt humiliated and was glad there was no one there to witness her shame.

Carla strode off with her back unnaturally straight and tears in her eyes. She would never forgive him. Yet she ached and remembered his kiss. He wasn't immune to her. If only she hadn't always to wear these boyish clothes! If only he could see her as she had been in that store! Her heart ached as much as her rear.

She brought the coffee in stony silence; she placed it carefully down beside him, fighting the urge to throw the hot liquid at his head. She did not see the softening in his eyes.

'Carla, be sensible.' He sighed. 'George loves you. He's shown that in so many ways. Why don't you become his woman?'

Her eyes pierced him like daggers and her lips curled.

'Because he's only half the man you are. He doesn't make my blood race as yours does. I'm not a whore who can lie with any man! Don't you understand?'

He sighed again. 'Then perhaps you should leave us, Carla. There's trouble comin' and it doesn't concern you or Joshua. Staying with us means that both of you are in danger.'

'I don't care. I'll fight for you. You're all I have in the world. If you die, I die. It's as simple as that!'

'Then you're goin' to have to remember you're a boy. I don't want you castin' sheep's eyes at me when George is around. I don't want trouble, Carla. I'm tellin' you straight, any more of this nonsense and you'll be left behind at the nearest town. I mean that, Carla, so take hold of yourself.'

She looked at his grim face, so unyielding, and slunk away.

Sabre heard her muttering to herself, slamming the frying pan around and taking it out on a jack rabbit she was chopping up for their next meal. He smiled and drank his coffee, his mind going back to his problem. He wondered just how much information those nosy Pinkerton agents had on them. Had they located Roscoe and the boys yet? If so, they could be their weakest link.

★　★　★

George Lucas was beginning to get anxious. He wasn't used to this hunting and tracking-down of animals for food. It was usually Johnny's job to do this.

He knew he couldn't slip through the undergrowth silently like Johnny. It took years of practise from childhood. Twice he'd spied two young deers and then, forgetting to get downwind, had alerted them and they'd bounded off into the unknown. He'd cursed, but both times he'd learned something new, never to move in a hurry and be careful about being in the right direction, windwise.

Then suddenly, without warning, he stumbled over a newly born fawn, lying in a nest of grass. He couldn't believe his luck. It looked at him with wide open innocent eyes and he hesitated. Christ! He couldn't bear to look into those eyes!

George Lucas knew that deep inside him he was a softie. The knowledge that made him flinch from hunting women, even though they deserved to die as spies and traitors, made him at variance with Sabre Wilde. They had clashed many times about his lifelong respect for the opposite sex and Sabre had taunted him times without number that his foolishness would get him into trouble some day. He was no survivor, Sabre had flung at him.

Now he knew he couldn't kill this baby, no matter how short of food they were. He moved backwards so that the tiny animal would not be alarmed. Then the crashing in the bushes began and he heard the alarm call of a raging mother. He turned swiftly as the female deer came charging at him. His reflex was sharp. His rifle came up and two shots slammed into the bony structure of her head. She reared and snorted, blood spurting. One shot had gone into one eye. She carried on drunkenly before she fell, her body heaving and then she lay slumped and still.

George took a deep breath. He hated himself at that moment. He looked at the helpless fawn. Goddammit! Why couldn't it have been some young stag he'd shot? Now the fawn would slowly die of starvation. He remembered the time they'd been hunting Pollyanna

Megrim, the spy who was sentenced to death by the President. Sabre Wilde had had his orders. He had been against her killing and it was he who'd had to shoot her. When she'd been engulfed by fire. He killed her to save her suffering. He thought of her as he turned on the fawn and shot it. A clean shot was better than days of dying or being mauled by another wild animal.

He shouldered the deer and without looking at the dead fawn made his way back to his tethered horse. He'd done enough killing for one day.

Back in camp, he dropped the carcass on the ground beside the camp-fire. He smelled coffee and his guts rumbled. He also smelled stew. Carla had been busy while he'd been away. He looked about him; Carla was absent. Probably washing her underclothes at the tiny stream. He whistled, and Sabre Wilde came into the clearing with a pile of wood in his arms.

'Hi, there! I was just gettin' worried about you.' Sabre grinned. 'I see you've been lucky. No sign of Johnny on your travels?'

'Nope. Not a sign of anyone and game's scarce in these parts.' He told Sabre ruefully about his experiences. 'I'll never make a hunting man, not like Johnny.'

'Well, you succeeded anyway and we can jerk some of the meat to take with us.'

'Where's Carla? I thought she would have been around with her butcher's knife at the ready.'

Sabre shrugged. 'Gone to bathe or somethin', she's havin' woman-trouble at the moment. We're goin' to have problems with that girl.'

George eyed him narrowly.

'In what way?'

Sabre hesitated before answering.

'She's got ants in her pants,' he finally came up with.

George Lucas stared at him.

'You mean . . . ?' He gulped out, not wanting to believe what he was hearing. The little bitch, he thought, stunned.

There he was, willing and agonizingly aware of her at every turn and she could turn on for this . . . this . . . ugly scarfaced *old man*! What had Sabre got that he hadn't?

He looked at Wilde with jealousy and loathing. 'Well? Go on, say it, goddam it to hell!'

Sabre viewed him with concern. 'Look, nothing happened. I sent her off with a flea in her ear. She's sulkin' somewhere.'

'I'll go and look for her.'

'*No!* Leave her alone!' Sabre snapped. 'Let her work this out for herself. If she rides with us, she must ride by my rules. As far as I'm concerned, she's just another man. Don't you get it? If we start treating her as a woman, she'll do for us all, and that goes for Joshua and Johnny as well. Even Johnny eyes her when he thinks no one's watchin'. If we're to survive in the situation we're in now, we must have no distractions. Right?'

'So you *do* find her attractive?'

'Yes, I suppose so. But it's just because it's a long time since I was with a woman. Goddammit, George, I'm human like the rest of us, but I'm not having her sex coming between us and what we're supposed to be doin'.'

'And what *are* we supposed to be doing at this time? The general's not given us any more assignments. Why?'

Sabre Wilde sighed. 'I don't know why, George, but if my instinct is anything to go by, I think there's been a change of policy.'

'You mean . . . ?'

'Yes, I think we're being hunted, not only to recover the gold we stashed away for just such an emergency, but for what we know. I think the President is wiping the slate clean before he leaves office.'

George whistled through his teeth.

'So we're genuine outlaws, banned from our families and now actually on the run and can be shot on sight!'

'Not shot until they recover the gold. After that . . . ' Sabre shrugged.

George Lucas reached for the coffee-pot and poured coffee in a tin mug.

'I feel like getting rip-roaring drunk!' He took several gulps of coffee and then said softly, 'What about Joshua and Johnny and Carla? It isn't fair keeping them with us. They don't need to suffer. We should warn them about what might happen.'

'I think the time's coming to put it to them. I wonder what's happened to Johnny. I thought he would have been with us by now. Josh's backtrackin' to see if he can find him. We can't get to hell out of here until they're back.'

'What about the gold?'

'That's another thing I wanted to talk to you all about. I think it's time we went back and dug it all up and shared it out. There's also vital papers belongin' to the President and to General Fothergill which I want. They could mean the difference between life and death. What will you do, George, if we split up?'

'Can we afford to split up? With the

gold we could go any place. Start again in Canada or go abroad . . . '

Sabre looked at him grimly. 'Look, if we're being betrayed by those bastards in Washington, I'm sure as hell not goin' quietly. There's Marcus Shane for one. He's the liaison officer between me and Fothergill. I want to know who's been dippin' his fingers into Treasury funds and buyin' guns and ammo and sellin' them to the Mexicans and Indians. You said yourself you didn't know Dan Tompkins when he said he was one of your father's agents. I'm stayin' around to do a bit of diggin'.'

'Well, if you're set on it, I suppose I will too.'

'Good, then that's settled. We get the gold, give the others their share and give them the choice to leave us if they want. Then you and I'll make for Arkansas and warn Roscoe and the boys.'

'Let's hope to God those Pinkerton agents haven't sniffed them out!'

'They'll have a job. Old Roscoe's a

wily bird. They're goin' to live mighty quiet for a while until the locals accept them for who they are.'

Late that night, after they had eaten and had bedded down for the night, Joshua brought in Johnny Eagle Eye with a bullet-wound in his shoulder.

Carla had returned, sulky and resentful, and had only grunted at George, but she'd been quick to butcher the carcass he'd brought in. She busied herself silently cooking stew and stripping the best meat and drying it over the fire. She'd kept her back to the men and didn't offer to look at Johnny's wound.

George examined it by the light of the fire but Joshua had done a good job. The bullet had gone straight through, so it only needed further cleaning and bandaging. Sabre watched, impatient to question Johnny. As he waited, he questioned Joshua.

'What happened? Did you find him shot or were you with him?'

'No. I recognized that pinto he rides.

It was grazin' and by the look of the grass around, he hadn't strayed far. It sure looked suspicious, boss and I reckoned Johnny wasn't far away. I found him under a bush, his wound caked black and flies hummin' around. I cleaned him up as best as I could and got him back here as fast as I could.'

'So you don't know who shot him?'

'He opened his eyes one time and muttered Max Berenger and then passed out again. I reckon he got too close and got careless. Not like Johnny to advertise his presence.'

'Hmm, we'll have to wait until he comes to, then. Mebbee he heard something Berenger didn't think he should.'

It was the next morning before Sabre heard about Max Berenger's rendezvous with Jack Vance, a noted go-between who passed himself off as a trader to the Comancheros and the Indians. When Berenger had mentioned Marcus Shane Johnny had become careless and bellied his way nearer to listen. His movement frightened a flock of birds, which alerted the men and he'd caught a bullet as he'd turned and run. But he remembered that something had been mentioned about Marcus Shane's boss.

'And you didn't hear his name?'

Johnny shook his head. 'Those birds flap their wings and squawk. I hear no words,' he said sadly. 'I grown old. I am ashamed of myself.'

'Look, Johnny, you did a good job,' Sabre consoled. 'You take it easy. We're goin' to have to leave you behind but we'll leave you some vittles to tide you over.' He looked around him. 'All of you, gather round. I have something important to say.'

They came and squatted around the fire.

'You too, Carla. It concerns everyone. The time has come to split up.' He waited while all took in his words.

'But we can't split up, boss!' Joshua burst out. 'Where would I be without you?'

'I'm sorry. But the fact is that I think

staying with me and George is putting you all in danger. You, Joshua and Carla and Johnny are not part of this trouble. It goes back to when we first robbed the train and took the gold.' He didn't mention the box of private papers. 'This was a military matter. It concerns a change of heart of this government. Once we were loyal servants of the President, now I have reason to believe he's set his own hounddogs onto us.'

George Lucas sat silent, listening and agreeing.

'But why?' Joshua asked, the whites of his eyes showing up against his black face. 'Why should he turn against you? You have done his biddin' at all times.'

'That's just it, Josh. I know too much. My usefulness is at an end. I'm an embarrassment to him.'

'So what are we supposed to do? Leave you and the captain here, to take your chances?'

'Yes. I propose that we all go back to where the gold is stashed, and I will give you three enough to see you comfortable for the rest of your lives. You can all start again, somewhere where you're not known.'

Johnny gave a short bitter laugh.

'I not go back to tribe. They stone me to death if I return, so where should I go if not with you?'

Sabre sighed. It was most difficult. 'It's your life I'm thinkin' of, Johnny.'

Carla, who had been sitting withdrawn and silent, now spoke up.

'And what am I supposed to do? A girl alone with some gold in her saddle-bags. I'll be either shot for the gold or taken as a whore. I don't want that, Sabre. You know my views. I don't want to be left behind!'

Sabre sat back on his heels and rubbed his chin, thoughts whirling, ideas coming and going. He was both touched and angry at the stubbornness of them all. He turned helplessly to George Lucas.

'Well? What do you think?'

George grinned. 'It seems you're

talking a lot of hot air! These folks have no one if they haven't got you. I envy you, Sabre, in lots of ways you don't know about.' He thought also of the loathing he'd felt for Sabre because of his own mad-headed obsession for Carla. 'You're just going to have to reconcile yourself to the fact that you've still got a gang behind you.'

'Then that's settled! The gold's become second priority. We head for Arkansas first and warn Roscoe and the boys. Then we go on back to Washington, and seek out Marcus Shane and make him talk.'

'Isn't that a bit risky? Going to Washington, I mean?' George asked.

'Washington's the last place whoever's huntin' us will expect us to be. Joshua, shave off my hair and beard, and you, Carla, cut off your hair and bind those breasts and turn yourself into a man, and what's more, think like a man!' He glared at her, knowing she would understand.

Her temper flared.

'I'll not cut my hair! Not for you or for anybody!'

He looked at her implacably.

'Very well. You don't ride with us. It is finished between us. I shall give you enough gold to make you a rich woman and not beholden to anyone. You will leave us at the next town.' He turned his back on her. They all stared at Sabre's stiff, uncompromising back.

'Sabre, you can't . . . ' began George.

Sabre turned around swiftly. 'I can. It is best for her and for us. If there are spies lookin' for us, what more likely than a bunch of men riding together with a woman in tow?'

'But she *looks* like a boy with her hair under her hat!'

'I said she must cut her hair and look like a man, not a boy. She must darken her chin and upper lip. We must all disguise ourselves or we'll never make Arkansas alive!'

'Aren't you being a little obsessive with this idea of yours, Sabre?' George was trouble. He didn't want Carla to leave them.

'Use your head, George and think it out for yourself. The agent, Tompkins, tied up with Max Berenger and Marcus Shane through the code name, Aloysius Dart. Don't you think that's ominous? How many folks know about our arrangement with the General through Aloysius Dart, huh?'

'Yes, when you think about it.' George scratched his head, still not convinced. 'I guess we'll have to go find Roscoe and see if those Pinkerton snoopers are sniffing them out.'

'Now you're talkin'. Josh, get your razor and mind how you shave me. I don't want cuts all over my head, and by the way, George, grow a moustache and get rid of those worn-out army pants you wear. We're goin' to travel on the rail-cars as a rancher with his boys goin' home after selling his herd, and you're the rancher. So dress the part.'

Carla listened and said nothing, then quietly crept away. Sometime later she came back to the fire, her eyes red with weeping, but her hair was cut short and she'd rubbed soot from the coffee-pot onto her chin and upper lip. From a distance it looked like a day's growth of beard.

The men gasped when they saw her, then laughed.

'Carla, I wouldn't have known you,' George spluttered. 'You've aged ten years!'

'It's not funny,' she flung at him. 'But if this is what I have to do to stay with you,' her voice wobbled, 'I'll do it!'

Early next morning they were packed up and ready to ride. It was hard leaving Johnny behind but he would follow them in a few days. He would be their eyes and ears for those who might follow them. They felt secure. He waved them goodbye and went to meditate and send them luck and protection on their journey.

They boarded a cattle-train coming out of Wichita for points south without incident. There were many cattle-ranchers making their way back home after selling stock in Wichita. It was a jovial crowd who spent their hours gambling and celebrating their success. Little heed was taken of the silent, tough-looking bunch in the last carriage before the horseboxes.

They were leading their horses off the train before it stopped steaming and were away before the rest of the now befuddled passengers. They were now heading for the Missouri and then on to Fort Smith, from where the way should be clear to Little Rock and Roscoe and the boys.

For the first time, Sabre's mood lightened. He was looking forward to seeing his old sergeant again. He'd missed the old devil more than he'd realized. He'd been the counter-balance to the captain's more youthful approach. Roscoe had sense. He hoped the old man was fit enough to travel with them.

He cast his eye over them all. There

was George, looking every inch the respectable rancher, and Carla, who was now wearing canvas pants, a checked shirt and a lambskin jacket that made her seem broader. Her hard black Spanish hat had been sacrificed for a dirty greasy Stetson and she wore a colourful bandanna about her neck. She looked the typical cowboy. Joshua had the look of an ex-slave, slightly downtrodden and servile, while he himself, he reckoned, with a black kerchief tied around his bald head and a makeshift eyepatch above the red puckered scar on his cheek, and his guns well to the fore, had turned himself into a rancher's foreman, tough and ready to fight in any bar-room brawl.

Gone was Major Horatio Wilde. Gone was Sabre Wilde, the outlaw. In their place was a fighting machine. He was confident that it would take a good Pinkerton to sniff him out.

4

'You're goddam sure of this man?' The long rangy-hard-faced man tapped the poster. The sheriff of Little Rock assumed he was a state marshal.

'Yessir! I could swear it on my old ma's grave! I saw the likeness as soon as I looked through the posters. The young 'un too, I can nearly swear it's the one called Skinner. I don't reckon on the rest and there's another boy with the old man. He reckons they're his sons. Name of Leary, Sam Leary. The boys are Duke and Mose. But they're all newcomers to Little Rock. Bought their place from old Shepperton's widder.'

'Do they come into town much?'

'Naw. Keeps theirselves to theirselves. They comes in for supplies and such and they have a beer but don't stay to cause any ruckus, like.'

'Have they hired hands?'

'Hell no. Place ain't big enough to carry extra men. Come to think of it, they seem to have a bankroll behind 'em. They don't aim to rear cattle or sheep. They don't even go to church!' He spat on the ground to show his disapproval.

'Right. They sound like the men we're lookin' for.'

'The reward will come to me?' the sheriff asked, hopefully. 'You wouldn't have found them but for me!'

'Look, what you think we issue posters for, mister? You're only doin' your duty as a sheriff should. If you get a reward for doin' your duty, then it's up to the big shots, not me. I'm only the hounddog who does all the work.'

The sheriff rubbed his bristly chin as the marshal slammed out of his office. Oh, well, it's none of my business, he reflected. At least he'd helped to capture two desperadoes, maybe three. He'd keep his fingers crossed about the reward and if he got it he would make damn sure his old woman knew nothing about it!

★   ★   ★

The Pinkerton agent who had posed as a state marshal drew rein at the top of a steep hill that ran down into a small valley. It was fertile with a small herd of cows grazing. Far below was the small ranch with a cluster of ramshackle barns and outhouses and a corral holding half a dozen horses.

He put his army field-glasses to his eyes and saw the tiny figure of a man sawing logs. It looked like a youth. Behind the watcher waited the six men he'd recruited for the job of taking out the two men he hunted.

All these men knew was that they were after wanted men and were getting paid for the job of capturing them and delivering them to the agent's boss, whoever he was. The agent was playing his cards close to his chest. The men only knew what they needed to know.

'Right, fellers, let's get the job done. We'll go in nice and cautious. I want them alive so no damnfool shootin' your heads off. Get it?'

The men nodded. Two men to take out, no sweat.

They rode down the winding trail in twos, with the Pinkerton man at the head. They were halfway to the ranch before the youth looked up from his sawing and ran into the ranch house to warn the others.

It looked as if taking out the two outlaws wasn't going to be as easy as they'd thought. A blast from a gun startled the horses which started to rear and dance. The Pinkerton man cursed.

'Hold your fire, boys and fan out. Two of you ride round the back to head 'em off if they try to run. The rest of you follow me.'

★ ★ ★

It had taken two weeks for Sabre Wilde and his riders to reach Little Rock via Fort Smith, crossing the Missouri and, after discreet enquiries, finding the location of Sam Leary's ranch.

They drew rein at the top of the valley. All was quiet except for the lowing of cattle and the odd scream of a hunting bird. Sabre narrowed his eyes as he saw the devastation around the ranch house. A thin black smoke still moved upwards from the remains of barns and storehouses.

Quickly he raised his glasses and cursed as he slowly took in the utter desolation. The ranch house was nothing but a mass of half-burned-out spars now turned to blackened charcoal.

'The sons of bitches got here before us!' he grated. 'We're too late!'

George Lucas eased his mount forward to stand beside Sabre and was handed the glasses.

'Look for yourself. What else could it be but those bastards in Washington settin' the hounds on to Roscoe. How in hell would they find him so quickly?'

'Use your head, Sabre. The powers that be in Washington would make full use of the telegraph wires. Let's go down there and look around. They'd want Roscoe alive, wouldn't they?'

Sabre took heart. Of course they'd want Roscoe and Skinner alive. If they were stubborn and denied knowledge of the location of the gold they would work on them until one of them cracked.

Sabre turned to the others, mouth tight, eyes smouldering.

'Let's go down there and take a look around. We could do with Johnny to read sign for us.'

They rode down the trail like a military charge, each of them apprehensive of what they might find.

It was soon apparent that the three men had been taken by surprise. They found Jodie's body strung up with two bullet-holes in chest and thigh. So the bastards had put pressure on to the others to make them talk, Sabre concluded.

'It looks as if they were taken from the back,' George called out as he probed the remains of the burnt-out buildings.

Carla and Joshua moved against the debris and found a couple of shotguns, looking as though they'd been tossed to one side. Both guns had been fired.

'They must have put up a fight before they were taken,' Joshua muttered to Carla.

'Yes, and here's an axe buried in a log. They must have been busy doing their chores, all peaceful-like and not expecting trouble.'

They buried Jodie and Sabre said a prayer over him. Joshua fashioned a rude cross from some of the burnt planks and placed it at the head of the grave.

'Jodie got killed on account of us. We promised him a new life with Roscoe and Skinner,' he said gruffly. He turned to face the grave. 'We'll not forget you,

boy. We'll get the bastards who did this.'
Then he turned to the rest of the group.
'Spread out, all of you and see which
way the sons of bitches left here. I want
to know whether they headed for
Washington or to the location of the
gold. Now get to it!'

★　★　★

Johnny Eagle Eye was travelling easily,
his eyes on the ground, looking for sign
of Sabre's mare's right back hoof. It
had a peculiarity about it that to Johnny
was like an open book. He also could
recognize the other horses' treads:
Carla's light weight and the way she
rode, her weight on one side, and the
captain's and Joshua's horses with their
own distinctive features. Putting them
all together it was like following
signposts all along the trail.

He knew who had stopped to relieve
himself or herself and when they'd
rested to give the horses a blow.
Although care had been taken to

obliterate all signs of their passing — fire scuffed out and covered with sand, and footprints and horses' hoof-prints brushed out — Johnny knew where they'd camped out and then moved on again.

It was second nature to him to look at the sky, watch the birds and check the wind; his sense of smell was sensitive enough to sniff a dead animal at a hundred yards.

He reined in at the top of the valley and saw them like small dots far below. They were moving around slowly as they examined the burnt-out ranch and its outbuildings. He'd never been here before and reckoned this was the place the old man and the two young men had chosen to make their home. He looked about him. It was a fair and fertile valley. A place where he could have made a home if he'd been so minded. But he, as an outcast from his tribe, was destined to wander.

He kicked his horse in the ribs and rode at a leisurely pace down below. His shoulder troubled him little now. It was healing well due to the mess of buffalo fat and herbs he'd slathered on it and, of course, the prayers that had been sung as he'd tended it.

Sabre heard his approach and stood up from searching the rubble. He smiled with relief and raised a hand in greeting. 'How!'

Johnny did likewise, then drew up and slid to the ground.

'What happened here?'

'They got here before us, Johnny. Thank God you're here to have a look around and see if we've missed any vital tracks. Roscoe and Skinner are gone but Jodie was tortured and shot. I want to know whether they're being taken to Washington or to Texas. How's the shoulder?'

Johnny shrugged, then raised his arm and twirled it about in response.

'Good as new, boss. I could do with some coffee and then I'll take a look-see. I've been out of coffee for days!'

He strode over to Carla who'd lit a

fire and was making panbread. She smiled at him.

'Good to see you, Johnny. Here, take a couple of these while I pour you coffee. There's honey in that sack.'

He wolfed down the food and drank two mugs of coffee. Then, without further ado, he joined those searching. But he went far beyond the perimeter of the buildings to search, noting each upturned stone and the disturbed earth. Then he called to them, using the sharp Apache signal that sounded part hawk and part owl. Sabre raised his head and came running.

'What is it? Have you found their tracks?'

Johnny grinned, took off his greasy black armyhat and scratched his head, then silently pointed.

There were not only new hoofprints, but a small piece of cloth which Sabre recognized as a strip from one of Roscoe's old army-shirts. The old devil had been smart. He'd left them a clue.

107

South! The bastards were going for gold instead of returning Roscoe and Skinner to Washington to face General Fothergill and whoever was using the general.

It also meant they wanted him, Sabre Wilde. They'd figured he would come after them for the two men's sakes. They trusted his and the captain's inbred gentlemanly instincts of loyalty to the men under their command, to attempt a rescue.

Sabre smiled wolfishly, showing strong white teeth in his tanned scarred face. Yes, he and Lucas would go after them, but not to fall into any trap.

He knew his worth to them and the danger. They couldn't bring him back to Washington. The scandal would be too great, especially at this time when the Republicans were on the move and the President's term of office was coming to a close.

No, it would be death for him and George Lucas as well as the old man and Skinner, once they had their hands on the gold and that strongbox . . .

Roscoe was a tough, wily old bird. Maybe he would withstand torture, but could young Ned? Ned Skinner regarded Roscoe as the father he'd never had. Could he watch Roscoe being tortured and not blurt out the location of that gold?

Sabre rasped his bristly chin. It itched. He pondered as he scratched, stale sweat pervading his nostrils. He sighed. He smelled like some tumbleweed drifter, and all because of that bastard up in Washington who'd ordered him into this way of life along with his most trusted men. Now their reward was to be hunted down like pariah dogs.

He strode back to camp. George and Joshua were waiting, their eyes now on him as they tried to guess his next move. Carla was silently packing up her equipment. She'd guessed already that they wouldn't be staying in this now desolate place.

'They've gone south,' Sabre barked.

'We'll track 'em as far as we can to make sure they're headin' to Texas. Then we hit the railroad and if possible get there before them. We'll clear the cache, fill the gap with stones and wait. Johnny's goin' ahead to beat out a trail for us. Joshua, round up as many horses as you can. They must have been in too much of a hurry to catch Roscoe's remuda when the corral fencing burned with the barns. The horses are still hangin' around, so they'll not be hard to catch.'

'We're not leaving *our* horses, Sabre?' George asked with concern. He'd had his mare for years and trusted her with his life.

'No, We'll ride two hours on and two hours off and save the horses. That way we can cover more ground. We might even catch up with the sons of bitches before we hit the railroad.'

He doubted it, for Jodie had begun to smell but not enough to bring down the vultures to tear at his body.

They were soon on their way. Johnny

had left a clear trail for them to follow. When they finally caught up with him he shook his head.

'They're travellin' fast, boss, and careless with it. Not trying to hide their tracks. They're leavin' a trail for us to follow.' He grinned, his teak-like face suddenly human. 'They must think we're loco, boss and don't know what they're up to.'

'You think they would lay a trap for us?'

'Yep. I figure that way, boss.'

'So we disappoint them. Let 'em wait for us, and go for the gold.'

'That's the way I see it, boss. Give 'em somethin' to worry about. They'll figure you make straight for Roscoe and Skinner.' He spat on the ground.

Sabre nodded.

'You're right, Johnny.' He raised his head and sniffed the air like a wolf. 'The sons of bitches haven't reckoned on me catchin' on to the real situation. We'll head straight for Texas.'

★ ★ ★

111

Roscoe groaned and tried to lift his head. It was too heavy for his shoulders. He heard a stifled moan close by and opened one bleary eye to find himself staring at Ned Skinner, still strung up by his arms to a post, his back a mass of red raw slashes where the blood had dried to a crusty black.

Roscoe dimly recalled the events of the day before, when he and Ned and Jodie had been surrounded by gunmen before they could lift a rifle to defend themselves.

Jodie had come to warn them of strangers but both he and Ned had been too far from the ranch house to get their guns. They'd been all peaceful-like, mending a corral fence, not expecting any strangers or trouble. That was the worst about living out in the wilds, one got lax and careless, thinking one'd never see violence again. But these bastards had known what they were doing. They were professionals. They knew their real names and all about Sabre and George Lucas. They also knew about the lost gold and how it should be returned to the Treasury.

Both he and Skinner had been stubborn and that was when they'd started on Jodie. It had been hard keeping his mouth shut when Jodie had started to scream, and it had been a relief when Jodie had broken free and made a run for it. He'd watched the boy being shot down.

It was then that Roscoe knew these men meant business; that even if he and Ned told them everything they knew they would never be left alive. His eyes had locked on to Ned's and he knew that Ned was aware of this too.

So they'd stayed mum and suffered for it. The thrashings seemed to have gone on for hours until at last a merciful oblivion had swallowed them both up.

Now Roscoe hurt whenever he moved a muscle. Suddenly the stable door opened, letting in early morning light. So he'd been unconscious all night. The man who stood over him had a bucket in his hand; the contents were flung over him and the icy cold water cleared his mind still further. He gasped and tried to shake his head; his shaggy grey hair was wet and it streaked across his eyes.

'Get up, you bastard and get out of here if you don't want to be burned alive!' The man turned to Skinner, cut the thongs about his wrists and tossed him like a bag of flour over one mighty shoulder. then, kicking Roscoe to his feet, he sent him sprawling outside the open door.

Roscoe, legs bowed and jelly-like, swayed and watched while a flaming torch was flung into the stable and the straw inside caught fire.

'You murderin' bastards!' Roscoe ground out and just had time to see more billowing smoke rising into the early morning air. He heard the frightened squeal of horses as they escaped through the unmended gap in the corral fence. At least they hadn't been caught by these sons of bitches, he thought, just before a blow to the chin floored him again.

He came to, slung over a horse's back, his hands tied together, his feet fastened loosely to the animal's girth. He groaned at each stride as the saddle dug into his belly. He must have vomited, for the sour stench of sickness was all about him. He wondered about Ned and hoped the boy was tough enough to survive. Then he lost consciousness again.

The Pinkerton agent looked at both his prisoners dispassionately. He had to keep them alive . . . for now. They were tough bastards, he had to give them their due. He'd studied the early file on Major Wilde's supposed defection and what followed after. He reckoned they had deliberately ridden south to Texas to infiltrate the other outlaw gangs in the badlands. It figured. He would have done the same in the circumstances. Therefore, they would carry that gold with them until they found themselves a hideout where it would be buried as an insurance if anything went wrong. That, too, was what he would have done in the circumstances.

So, he had to be right. They would travel openly and slowly, hoping Sabre Wilde might come after them to save his two men, or if he did the less likely thing and made for Texas, he was confident they would get on his trail there. Sabre Wilde would surely come after them in Texas. Either way, they would get him. After all, Sabre Wilde didn't know the true situation in Washington.

He smiled as he thought of the hunter hunted. He wanted to see Wilde's face when he realized he'd been betrayed. By whom? That last piece of the puzzle had not been explained to him and it niggled him. Many times he'd run through what he did know and tried to make a guess. It couldn't be the President himself or that mangy old General Fothergill. Or could it? Even old men had their secrets. His thoughts roamed over several other close members of the White House. Who else could be involved in that conspiracy? It had to do with the Treasury, that was for sure, or they wouldn't have access to the gold. There was Berny Rotherheim, the minister of Internal Financial Affairs and his penpushing pals, but old Berny was just a dried-up mathematician with his head in the clouds. His world was all about numbers and balancing books. He dismissed him as being ludicrous. He sighed. Maybe he would never know the real outcome of this particular assignment. Meanwhile he had to watch his back.

★　★　★

They were making good time and Sabre was pleased with their progress. They had many miles to travel but now were heading for a new spur line. It seemed that the railroad bosses were branching out in all directions. Sooner or later they would come to a junction and they could board the first train going south.

It was Joshua who spotted the smoke in the far distance. It ran along the horizon in grey puffs, not like a building burning or an Indian signal. This smoke moved in a straight line.

'Look, boss,' Joshua pointed. 'Engine smoke!' Sabre nodded.

'We're in luck, boys. They're layin' track and if we catch up with them we can ride to their next stopping-point.'

They came across a temporary town, consisting of rows of tents with one large one which was the dining-tent for the railroad workers. The men were dirty and the ground was ploughed up into muddy ruts. There was a line of small tents tucked away from the rest. They were for the Happy House girls, the followers who grafted on to any man who had the money to pay. The rest of the population were rough workers, itinerants who had no ready cash and so worked their way over the continent.

A portly man in nearly new breeches and riding-boots and smoking a big fat cigar accosted them as they rode in.

'Hey, mister, I see you've got extra horses. You want to sell? I'm Joe Healey and I'm contracted to keep the supplies rollin' down the line. The train's late. It should have rolled yesterday but we're short of packhorses to clear the rest of the tents and baggage for the men. The railroad bosses pay well for horses and equipment and if you take responsibility for the goods on the horses' backs you get paid too. How about it, feller?'

Sabre glanced at George Lucas and their eyes met. This couldn't be better. They'd get free travel on the train and be absorbed amongst the other passengers and, better still, they'd not be travelling *with* them. They would bed down amongst the horses and the packs in the stock-cars.

He held out his hand.

'Sure, mister, it's a deal. We'll pack

our stuff on our own animals, and the ten left over are yours. What's your price?'

His eyebrows rose at the price offered.

'Sure. They're not made of gold, but I'll not argue with that. If that's your goin' price, I'll take it like a shot!'

'You boys lookin' for work in Texas? You're a pretty mixed bunch.' Healey's eyes slid over to Joshua and Carla and Johnny and he frowned a little as he studied George Lucas. 'You buddies from the war?' he asked, taking in Johnny's army hat. He reckoned to know an Indian scout when he saw one.

'Yeah, you might say that. We're buddies and stick together. We reckon mebbe to get us a ranch and breed us some good cattle. They say there's much good land still to be had, if you fight for it.'

Healey looked at him hard.

'You and that feller,' nodding to Lucas, 'look like military men. You wouldn't like to work for the railroad until we hit the Sante Fe track? You and the others would earn yourselves a useful stake. We're short of men who can organize. The last supplies boss got hisself shot up over a crap-grame and a couple of crazy bastards scarpered when the railroad police came lookin' for escaped convicts. Yeh, we could do with some new blood. How about it?'

Sabre shrugged his wide shoulders. He didn't like the words railroad police. Not that he thought the hunt for them would be made public. But something could happen and they could be exposed to the brunt of any rough stuff. There weren't many bunches of men with a former negro slave and onetime Indian scout amongst them. Of course they'd be looking for a woman with them but Carla had done a mighty fine job of posing as a youth, hardly old enough to have a fuzz on his face. But one wrong move from her, and all hell could break loose.

'Thanks for the offer, mister. We only go as far as Tonkawa.'

'Where the hell's that?'

'Down beyond the Colorado River.'

'So you've plenty ridin' to do after you leave us. A pity. But you'll get your arses rested a mite on the way.'

'We'll help set up your next end-of-line town and the next, but we'll leave when the time comes, if that's all right with you?'

'Yeh, a bit of help is better than no help. Right, from now on you're on the payroll. Grub's all in and you can start by packin' those horses with all those supplies yonder. Then board the horses on the stock-cars. The driver's boilin' mad that he couldn't get goin' yesterday.' The little man stumped off, a cloud of cigar smoke whirling about his head.

Eventually the engine's whistle blew, and a puff of grey-black smoke shot from the smoke-stack. The wheels squealed and groaned and the two closed carriages with the heavily laden stock-cars moved slowly ahead. They were on their way.

⋆ ⋆ ⋆

The Pinkerton agent couldn't understand why Sabre Wilde didn't ride to the rescue of the old man and the youth. That said how much loyalty Wilde felt for his men, he concluded. He taunted the two men cruelly with the news that their much revered boss had let them down. He wasn't coming to attempt a rescue. Roscoe and Ned Skinner lay quietly listening to the man's insults, their eyes half closed to hide their anger. The stupid bastard! He didn't know a thing about loyalty. Sabre Wilde wouldn't leave them to rot. He would have some plan . . . They listened, mute, as would men who were hardly conscious. They were biding their time. Neither man was as helpless as he made out. Skinner's back was red-raw and the flies sucked at his crusted blood. It was hell to move but like hell would he show it!

He knew as did Roscoe that while they kept mum they would be kept alive. If they talked, then it would be a matter of whether the son of a bitch had orders to kill them. They were under no illusions. This feller was a killer.

⋆ ⋆ ⋆

The train trundled fifty miles ahead along the newly laid track. The rails gleamed in the sun. Then they came upon teams of men hauling sleepers, cutting down trees, stripping them of branches, shovelling dirt for foundations. The train's brakes squealed and it came to a shuddering stop.

The men watching its arrival cheered. Some even threw their caps in the air. Now there would be new supplies, kegs of ale and soon, when the new tents were erected, the women would arrive and the foremost teams of railmen who'd roughed it for weeks would be able to relax while new teams took over.

They could drink and gamble and fornicate, spend some of their hard-earned cash and become human once again.

Sabre Wilde found there was an art in supervising the erection of the new tents. He had to administer rough justice as arguments broke out amongst the men. Carla stayed close to him. Already she'd suffered a couple of advances from men who thought she was a pretty boy, but her wildcat fighting ability and her sharp knife had cooled their ardour. She was quite capable of slitting a man's belly wide open or going for his throat.

They backed off. There was more to this pretty boy than his looks.

Once the town was established they moved on with the packhorses, following the marked-out route the railroad would follow. The surveyors had marked the way with a series of small flags which a rider had to watch over, moving ceaselessly up and down the marked way to look out for interference from hostile Indians. Sabre was ordered to leave certain supplies along the way for the men working as the railtracks moved slowly onwards.

It was after the second end-of-line town was erected that Sabre recognized certain bluffs. They were nearing the vicinity where the gold was stashed.

He warned the overseer that they were coming to the end of their service.

'Well, you've all done a good job. I only wish you'd been goin' all the way, but you warned me.' He handed over a wad of notes and a small sheet of paper. 'You'll find it all there, your wages and the price we agreed for the horses. I'm obliged to you, and if your prospects don't turn out right, you know where to look for a job! Good luck to you all!' He bustled off as if he had no time to waste.

Sabre looked after him.

'I wonder how much he's makin' out of the railroad?' he asked reflectively.

126

'Enough to set him up for life, I should think,' George Lucas answered, then he grinned at Sabre. 'He'd be a fool if he didn't!'

They repacked their own horses and soon they were riding away from the railroad. For the first time in weeks, Sabre felt free again and the smell of men and engine-smoke was out of his nostrils. He sniffed appreciatively.

'God, it's great to get into the real open spaces once more. The next stop's the hideout and let's hope we're there before Roscoe and young Ned!'

A touch to the ribs and Sabre Wilde's horse lengthened her stride, the others following close behind. Two days' ride and they would be there.

5

'Come on, feller, don't be a fool!' The agent glared at Roscoe's bloody face, noting the faraway look in the man's eyes. Christ, he'd better be careful. The old man might take some kind of seizure and drop dead and he didn't want that. If all else failed and Wilde, goddamn him, failed to fall into the net, he had to take him and Skinner back to Washington to prove he'd done what he could and let the big nobs work them over. Skinner he looked at with contempt. The youth had no guts. He'd flaked out after the fifty strokes of the whip and wouldn't be coherent for the next twelve hours.

'Well, answer me, goddammit! Playin' hero will get you nowhere. We've got files on you fellers. We know the hideout's in Texas, but Wilde was too sly to give away the location even to his buddy

Aloysius Dart, God bless him! Where's the place, mister? Open your mouth and tell me or I'll close it for ever!' He shook Roscoe until his teeth rattled.

Roscoe roused himself a little when he heard the name Aloysius Dart. It was as if he wasn't aware of the man crouched over him.

'Aloysius Dart,' he whispered. 'I'll see that bastard in hell!' His head fell back and his eyes closed.

The Pinkerton man stood upright and gave Roscoe a kick in the ribs.

'The ornery old bastard! Chuck a bucket of water over him,' he said to one of the men gathered around them. 'The old goat won't get the better of me.' He looked at Ned Skinner lying slumped on the ground. 'And throw a bucket over that stubborn mother-sucker too. Goddammit to hell! I'm not goin' to be bested by this trash! We've come a long way and I'm not givin' up now!'

He walked away while two men hastened from the camp to the small stream close by and brought back two battered buckets of water to swish over the two men.

The cold water was like a powerful jet in the face. Roscoe groaned and opened his eyes. The men laughed to see the shock on both faces. Then a hand snaked out, caught an ankle and pulled. Ned Skinner rolled and brought the man down before either man was aware of what was happening. Then Roscoe took a dive for the other man and butted his legs with his head.

It was all over in a very few minutes. A muscular jab to the jaw from Ned and his man was out cold. Roscoe hung on to the other thrashing man until Ned turned; a hard kick to the head quietened the other.

Ned heaved himself to his feet a little drunkenly. His back ached with every movement, but he was not as hurt as he'd made out. Roscoe rose to his knees, dizzy now with the exertion.

'Help me,' he muttered. Ned swung him upright, then heaved him on to one broad shoulder. He was going to make a run for it.

He crouched low and made for the line of tethered horses. Thank God they'd never been unsaddled. He heaved Roscoe across the one at the end of the line, unloosened its head-rope and, speaking softly to it, led it away and into the brush. There he climbed aboard and, holding Roscoe firmly in front of him, walked softly away and out of earshot. Then he let the horse go with a mighty kick to the ribs.

Roscoe stifled a groan. It was worth the pain to be free. After a while he said painfully,

'You know where you are, son?'

'Yeh, you might say that.'

'Then stop and let me make myself comfortable. I want to piss!'

Ned Skinner grinned.

'You and your bladder! Why don't you just let it go?'

''Cos it smells, you durned fool!'

'You stink already, Roscoe. Piss won't

131

make much difference!'

'I just don't like the smell of it! Now take buffalo-fat, I don't mind that or even a bit of stale body-sweat, but piss, no! I'm particular.'

They stopped and rested and made themselves comfortable. A lot of the dried blood on both of them had been washed away with the water but both knew that in this heat, what with the flies and that, they must get cleaned up soon or infection would set in.

Their stomachs were also grumbling. Their captors had not been lavish with the food they'd shared. It was imperative to get to the hideout where there was always a stash of food staples. There would be coffee and sugar and meal and dried beans and tins of peaches and anything that would keep, along with an armoury of guns and ammunition.

It was just a matter getting there before the Pinkerton agent could catch up with them. They had the advantage. They knew where they were going. The agent did not.

Sabre Wilde, with the others gathered around him, paused on the ridge going down into the hollow and carefully looked around. Nothing moved, no birds fluttered as if disturbed.

The hollow looked as it had when they'd moved out months ago. They'd only been back once in the years they'd been on the owlhoot trail.

It was a quiet peaceful place, studded with cacti and sagebrush and stunted trees. It held a secret that only those who'd taken time to explore the place could know. Half-way up the steepest side of the bowl was a small opening, now swamped by clinging bushes even thicker than they remembered. That small opening led into a vast cavern let into the side of the steep incline.

Sabre reckoned that in ages past it had been the home of wandering people, perhaps used during wars between tribes, a place to hide the women and children. Inside, after one got through the small aperture, which was just as high as a horse, the cave opened out into a vast rocky area, capable of housing at least twenty men and a dozen horses.

'Right, everything seems quiet. No visitors yet. We'll get on down.'

While the others waited, Sabre climbed up to the opening of the cave, noting no disturbance. He broke through the new growth and looked inside. All was quiet.

He waved.

'All clear, you can all come up. Follow each other and leave as little disturbance as possible.'

Carefully they climbed, helping their horses over the difficult parts. Johnny came last, carefully brushing hoofmarks away with a branch of sagebrush.

Sabre had found a torch near the entrance and lighted it. The flames flared and flickered as they looked around. It smelled damp and earthy but the floor was dry and there was no indication that it had become a lair for a wild animal.

He grinned with relief.

'Well now, I reckon we can rest easy. Carla, you make up your bed where you did before at the back, while we sort ourselves out here in front. And while you're back there, Carla, check the provisions and see if there is any spoilage. We could do with a fire, Joshua. We could use some of the stack of firebrands we left. We can gather fresh wood tomorrow.' He stretched. 'We're due for a decent meal, Joshua. See what you can cook up.'

They settled in to wait. Johnny elected to forage around and see if he could snare a rabbit or some other small animal. He would dig pits later to catch large animals or even men who might creep up on them. He had much work to do . . . at sundown he must go to commune with his gods.

George Lucas checked the ammunition in its strongboxes and found it undamaged. Then he broke open the cases containing the rifles and was satisfied they were protected from damp. Each had been oiled and cleaned before being stashed away. They were ready for a siege.

One thing was lacking in the cave. Water. They needed water in the drums they'd left behind. They were now rusty and needed cleaning. That would be a job for Joshua. For now, Sabre would go to the stream that ran in the next draw and carry back, in an Indian skin called a parfleche, what they would need for the moment.

The stream in the next draw was probably the reason why no one ventured into the small hollow. It did not invite exploration. Who would camp there when there was a good stream in the next draw?

They spent their first night in comfort. Bellies full, camp-fire doused so that the cave wasn't filled with smoke, a two-hour watch was kept by each man in turn. Carla slept fitfully. She'd never liked sleeping in caves. It was too claustrophobic for her. But she endured in silence. She knew from experience that to complain was to accentuate her femininity. To them she was just another man, except for George, of course. She knew of his longing for her, and his lusting after her triggered off her own lusting after Sabre. She sighed and turned over restlessly. If it hadn't been for the fact that she had nowhere to go and no other friends but them, she would have gone long since. As it was, she regarded them as family.

Without them, the world would be an alien, dangerous place.

George Lucas greeted the dawn by going outside and breathing deeply, opening his trousers and urinating over the matted bushes.

The sun was up. It was going to be another scorcher, but now it was relatively cool. It was good to be alive. After buttoning up he scrambled downhill. He might as well start the business of gathering fresh wood before the heat of the day. Inside the cave all was still quiet. Only Johnny was missing. He never slept inside. George reckoned he'd be perched on some rock somewhere, cross-legged, hands outstretched to the rising sun and muttering whatever it was he muttered to his gods. A queer feller, Johnny Eagle Eye, so fierce and yet so gentle, someone he'd never really understood. But they would fight and die for each other, that was for sure. George smiled as he wandered between thickets picking up dead wood. He liked the early mornings. They gave him a kind of peace, reminding him of the carefree days of his youth when all he had to worry about were his social obligations. It had seemed important to be successful in the polite graces, how to treat a young lady, to flatter and promise much with his eyes and gestures and yet know when to draw the line.

It all changed when he joined the

army. It had been a mixture of discipline and protocol. One had to please the officers' wives. One day those same wives might influence their husbands on his advancement. Then it had been imperative to marry when he became captain. Now he could hardly remember what his intended bride had looked like.

Those were far-off days. Reality was more brutal. Reality was why he liked this time on his own, to remember, to become human once again. He looked down at himself and saw the dirty sweat-soaked figure, felt the bristled chin and sighed. He'd not realized what he would lose when he'd volunteered with Major Wilde to obey the President's orders and deal out justice to the traitors of the Union.

He turned to go back to the hidden camp when he heard a yelp as if someone somewhere was caught up on the hellish hooks of the cactus. He dropped his load and crouching, pulled his gun and crept forward. Was it an animal or was it a human, and if a man why was he here skulking in the brush?

He stopped to listen. All was quiet. He held his breath, cold prickles running down his back. He bent and groped for a rock and flung it far ahead of him. Immediately came a flurry of birds into the air. His breath blasted from him. What he'd heard could have been the death rattle of some beast crashing to its knees. If this was so, its predator would be close by.

He turned away. Whatever was out there could carry on with the grisly business. He hadn't his rifle with him to confront a mountain cat.

Then suddenly he stopped dead in his tracks. He'd heard a distinct curse as a man at the end of his tether and angry with himself.

He listened. The muttering came again. He moved slowly and cautiously in the direction of the sound. Who in his right mind would be wandering alone in this godforsaken country? Or could it be one of the President's bloodhounds on their tracks, who'd got separated from the rest of the pack?

Step by step he moved forward, careful to put his feet down lightly and not crack any dead wood lying underfoot, as Johnny had taught him. He blessed Johnny and his fieldcraft. The way was leading him into that draw where the stream ran and then meandered away into the distance. Whoever was out there must have followed the stream. But why leave it unless he was looking for their hideout?

He lay belly down and looked over a ridge that was partly covered with giant cacti. Any man trying to break through that lot had a big heart in his belly.

Then he spotted movement. He waited. He wished he'd had his field-glasses with him to see who the stranger was.

Then to his amazement he saw a crouching figure emerge, scratched and bleeding and dragging at a bundle on the ground. What in hell . . . ?

As he watched he saw the man straighten up and stretch his back muscles, and then, cursing softly, bend and start dragging again.

Then all was clear. It was a man being dragged along the stony ground. George Lucas drew a sharp breath. The early sunlight had caught the man, full face. It was Ned Skinner!

'Skinner! Private Skinner! Do you hear me?'

Ned Skinner looked around, startled. He was in the process of diving back into the cactus thicket when he heard George shout again.

'It's Lucas, Ned. For Chrissake don't go back into that hellish jungle!'

Then he stood up and ran down the slope towards Ned, who sank to his knees and began to cry.

'Ned, you're safe, Ned. Hold up, boy. I'll get you back to the camp.' All the while he was squatting over Roscoe who lay with his eyes closed. There was a bullet-hole in Roscoe's arm which had bled profusely.

Ned raised a head too heavy to hold up.

'I did the best I could for him, Cap. I thought we'd got away but they followed and Roscoe caught it. I held on to him and we got away. They're following close behind. The blood, you know . . . it keeps drippin' and those devils are lookin' for it. I ditched the horse and carried him into the cactus. I figured they wouldn't have the guts to follow . . . ' Ned sighed. 'It's been a long time. I'm all tuckered out . . . ' He collapsed beside Roscoe.

George Lucas was in a quandary. He couldn't move both men together. All he could do was hide Skinner and carry Roscoe back to camp first. Roscoe looked in dire need of help, if it wasn't already too late.

He started to drag the unconscious Skinner into the shade of a sagebrush. Skinner opened his eyes briefly, groaned and slumped again into oblivion. God knows how long he'd been carrying Roscoe and beating his way through the thick fleshy cactus. Torn clothes and deep scratches testified to his endurance.

He returned to Roscoe and was squatting to gather him up in his arms when he became aware of something. The hair on the back of his neck prickled. His hands fell away from Roscoe as he tensed to face what was behind him.

Then Johnny Eagle Eye put a light hand on his shoulder.

'Relax, Cap. I saw you from up yonder.' He pointed to a far hillock. George Lucas sighed with relief.

'Jesus Christ, Johnny, you're like a cat! I nearly crapped myself. You've cost me a life! Hell's bells! I'm glad I'm your friend! You're just in time to help me with these guys. We'll get 'em back to camp, pronto. I think poor Roscoe's had it.'

Johnny bent down and examined Roscoe briefly. He put his hand to the old man's mouth and nose.

'No breath. Roscoe hover between

earth-plane and hunting-ground. He in limbo. Maybe we can call him back.'

'Then you take him back quickly to camp, Johnny, while I see to Ned. I'll follow as soon as I get him upright. He's a big man to carry.'

It took a while for George Lucas to manoeuvre Private Skinner upright. His legs were like jelly. He was all in but, at last, leaning heavily on Lucas, Skinner finally made the effort to partly walk and partly be carried to the camp.

There Lucas found Carla and Sabre tending Roscoe, but, with all their efforts, Roscoe did not recover. He had lost too much blood.

Carla turned her attention on Skinner. A shot of whiskey and then a bowl of cornmeal hastily prepared, helped to bring him round and put some strength into his exhausted muscles. Carla bathed his cuts and revealed quietly to Sabre that both men had been whipped. The criss-cross whip-marks showed clearly on both backs when the blood was washed away.

145

Sabre's mouth hardened into an unforgiving line.

'The bastards!' he said between gritted teeth. 'For what we sacrificed our lives and honour for! I'm goin' back to Washington and I'll ferret out the man behind all this. I can't believe it's the President alone. There's more to it than that. I want to know who set up all this and if General Fothergill's involved, I'll have his balls . . . '

'You can't go back,' George Lucas protested. 'They'll shoot you before you get there!'

'It's that strongbox they want. That more than the gold. As soon as Skinner is fit enough to travel, we'll head out and dig up that gold. It will be shared out and then we'll split up. No good you all dodgin' the Feds all your life. It's not fair on you, George. It's me they want. Skinner and Joshua and Carla can disappear and make new lives for themselves. Meanwhile we've got to bury Roscoe, poor devil. I'm sorry it had to come to this.'

Sabre spoke bitterly. He hadn't told George Lucas all that was in his mind. It was going to be one man's war against those responsible and if the President was implicated in the whole rotten mess, then he would bring him down . . .

The grave was dug and Roscoe was buried. Sabre spoke some words over him and a rough cross was dug into the ground at his head. He lay partly concealed under a spreading sagebrush. The ground had been dug deep enough for no marauding animals to be able to dig him up.

Three days later, they moved out. They were on the way to the location of the gold, and of the strongbox.

★ ★ ★

The Pinkerton man cursed. They'd followed the fugitives easily by the copious bleeding. But then suddenly there had been only the horse's hoofprints to follow. No bleeding.

Therefore the old man must have snuffed it and Skinner had tossed the body into a crevice and they'd missed signs of it.

It had been one of the trackers who'd finally come up with another solution. He was loath to air his idea, for this Washington spyman was foul-tempered and made a man feel a fool.

'Look, that there horse isn't runnin' in a straight line. He's wandering, and another thing his hoofs don't dig into the ground like they did. I think that horse is runnin' free!'

He waited for an explosion of incredulous temper. It came.

'Don't be a fool! No man's goin' to free his horse in this wilderness unless it's lame and that one sure isn't! Use your brains, feller, if you have any. Even I know a man dies in this goddamned country if he loses his horse.'

The tracker looked thoughtfully at him.

'You seem to know it all, mister,' There was a snigger behind the words

148

which infuriated the spyman more. 'Tell me, mister, what *you* think happened, then?'

'I don't know! That's what you fellers are paid for.'

'Well then, I'm tellin' you that horse is runnin' free!'

The agent took off his hat and scratched his sweaty head. He was sticky and his arse was sore and he'd run out of whiskey and he wished he was back on the streets of Washington. He'd thought he'd be a match for any country bumpkin any day but now he was beginning to think he'd bitten off more than he could chew. He daren't think of the consequences if he made for nearby civilization, found a telegraph office, contacted Aloysius Dart, whoever he was, and confessed to failure. Hell, they'd have his guts. He'd been so sure it would be an open and shut case. Merely a case of running down an unsuspecting bunch and bringing them back to Washington with the gold and that strongbox that all the fuss was about. He sweated more as he thought of the laughing-stock he would be amongst the other Pinkerton men and the rage he would face from those unknown pen-pushers . . .

'Look, we'll spread out. You, Ben, follow that horse trail and we'll take a looksee over the hill. That young feller wouldn't have the guts to make away through that sea of cactus. No, he'd make for some easy going. There must be some trail we've missed in this cursed country. Anyone finding anything, shoot three times into the air and we'll come runnin'.'

★ ★ ★

Johnny rode point, with the others a hundred yards behind. Every now and again Johnny would spur his horse and ride ahead when the ground rose. He would take a careful look around for any movement, noting bird patterns and watching for faint plumes of smoke that might betray any hidden camp.

Meanwhile, Ned Skinner recounted what had happened at the ranch and how they'd been taken by surprise. Jodie had warned them too late. Sabre told him how they had found him and buried him. Ned shook his head.

'Poor Jodie. He was a great kid and we had such plans with old Roscoe. We were goin' to build up a decent herd, and now . . .' He broke off, shaking his head, eyes blinking.

Sabre reached out and patted his shoulder.

'Look, Ned, you're young enough to start again. There's the gold. You can go anywhere you like and start fresh.'

'It won't be the same, boss. I guess I'll be stickin' with you.'

Sabre shook his head.

'It won't do, boy. Anyone stickin' with me will run the same danger. They want me. I've got the papers they want. This is not just about a gold stash. That's the excuse. When we dig this gold up and I get the strongbox, I'm goin' through those papers with a fine-tooth comb. There's somethin' more than I first figured. I'm sure of it.'

'What you reckon it is, boss?'

'What else but bribery and corruption in high places?' Sabre said it grimly. 'But there must be somethin' to show me where the danger's comin' from.'

'I'll stick with you, boss. You'll need all the help you can get.'

They rode on.

They turned into a canyon, rugged with jagged rocks sticking up like teeth. There was very little vegetation and the sun beating down made it like a hell-hole. It was known in the old days by the Indians as the Cauldron of the Underworld, for in its midst a great muddy lake simmered and bubbled. Rising from it was a sulphur-smelling steam that every now and then exploded, sending a stream of hot mud far and wide.

There were no birds in that canyon. Indeed, except for lizards lying under the shade of small boulders and rocks, nothing else stirred.

Joshua shivered, rolling his eyes. He felt the evil vibrations of this place. Carla sat straight on her mount, a trickle of sweat running down both cheeks and between her breasts. She too was uncomfortable but refused to show a sign. It would be good to find what they'd come for and get out of this place.

They rode by the bubbling lake and came to a jumble of rocks. It was as if a giant hand had tried to build a fort and failed, leaving a pile of debris behind.

Johnny was waiting for them. He'd already climbed to the top of the heap and taken a look around. Nothing stirred. Now he was below and waiting.

Sabre dismounted and the others followed. All conscious of the fierce heat of the sandy floor, Sabre pulled his hat well over his eyes. His throat was parched. He needed a drink but he would wait until all could drink. They were carrying canteens of water, for there would be no water in this canyon.

He stretched, conscious of his sweat.

'We'll make camp, bed down early and start diggin' an hour before dawn. Then we'll get out of this hell pronto. Joshua, look to the horses. Get 'em into shade and feed 'em grain and water them sparely. We can't afford to waste a drop.'

'Yessir!' Joshua gathered up the reins of the horses. He led them into a small crack in the rocks which turned into a small cave but with the blue sky showing far above. The horses whinnied and protested, but when the first one moved in, the rest followed.

There was no camp-fire, for there was no wood for fuel, so they made do with stale bread and dried meat and water to wash it all down.

After eating, Sabre and George Lucas went to locate the stash site. Nothing had been disturbed. George turned over a couple of rocks and found the shovels they'd left behind. He grinned.

'Looks like it'll be easy pickings,' he said with a laugh, hauling out the shovels and striking at the sandy earth.

'Mm, well let's wait and see,' Sabre muttered. It could seem too easy.

Sabre spent a restless night. He had the others up well before dawn. It was still hot and humid, but nothing like it would be later in the day. He reckoned with all of them doing a stint of digging, the haul could be shifted in four hours and they could be riding out of the canyon well before noon.

The digging was harder than Lucas estimated. It was rock hard but gradually they got down to the first crate and that gave them heart. They redoubled their efforts and soon they had the boxes lifted. Only the strongbox remained. This proved harder to shift than the rest but eventually it was heaved out. They stood panting as they surveyed the loot.

Each of them had dreams of the future, when this should all be over. Only Sabre regarded the chests as a liability rather than a windfall. This and the strongbox were the reasons why they were being hunted like dogs.

The crates were broken open. The gold, in bags, was shared equally and stashed in saddle-bags so that each of them was responsible for his own. Sabre took charge of the strongbox. Once out of the canyon he would take out the papers, hide the box and study the contents at leisure.

They watered the horses, ate a scratch meal and took a small drink each. Then they prepared to leave the canyon.

* * *

There was panic in the White House. A secret meeting had been arranged by the President. The gold had not been retrieved and certain discrepancies in the financial budget would be found. Soon, his term of office would be over and the scandal of those discrepancies would be made public.

There were also other problems facing those present. Certain matters, not covered by the President's plan to deal initially with his enemies and that he was not aware of, had now to be faced. Matters concerning bribes and illicit sales of arms and ammunition and supplies, which had been operating all through the war. There had been interchanges between the Rebels and the Yanks, which had been instrumental in keeping the war effort going. Indeed it had been to the advantage of those involved to keep the war going. Those who trafficked had grown rich. Now it could all come to an end in public scandal. The latest news was that the two prisoners who could have led them to Sabre Wilde had escaped.

The fool of a Pinkerton agent had been reprimanded and disgraced but that didn't help the situation now.

General Fothergill listened to the arguments but was silent. He had always disapproved of the President's plan to use Major Wilde and his men, but he had carried out orders and been the liaison between Wilde and the President.

He thought of the man who had intercepted the Aloysius Dart communications and relayed them to him, who in turn kept the President informed. Something smelt. He wanted to warn the major but it looked at the moment as though he couldn't trust anyone. Major Wilde had gone missing, no doubt under cover in the role he'd adopted so well.

He listened but kept his thoughts to himself. He only hoped Wilde wouldn't try to contact him through Aloysius Dart.

* * *

Once the canyon was behind them the going got easier. They moved into grasslands as they neared the Colorado River. They all relaxed a little and grew more cheerful.

But that night in camp, Sabre put it straight to them all.

'I said before and I'm saying it again, we must split up. You, Carla, can make your way down to Mexico and start a new life. You've got the means to buy yourself a ranch or marry a don, whichever appeals to you. Joshua, what do you intend to do?'

Joshua shrugged. 'I've no family. I'd just as soon stick with you. You know that, boss.'

'It'll be dangerous staying with me. That's why I want you all to scatter. They're after me. Don't put your life on the line because of mistaken loyalty, Josh. You could go north and seek out one of the new towns that's sprung up for coloured people. You've got the know-how to help a new community and the gold to do it.'

Joshua shrugged bowed shoulders. 'It would be like losin' ma family.'

Sabre sighed. 'What about you, George? Have you made your mind up to split with us? For God's sake be sensible and say yes!'

George Lucas coughed and looked at

Carla. Sabre knew what was going through his mind. Poor George, carrying a torch for Carla who didn't seem to know he existed as a man, only as a useful member of the gang.

'I haven't made my mind up, Sabre. I can't go back to my family. I'm dead as far as they're concerned, and as far as making a new life away from you all, I can't see it, unless of course I was asked to go to Mexico.'

Carla sniffed. 'Who'd ask you to? I'm not going to no Mexico! I've no one down there I want to see again! A pox on Mexico!'

Sabre sighed, got to his feet and walked away, his emotions stirred by the evidence of loyalty. The responsibility for keeping them alive was lying heavy on him.

Again he cursed General Fothergill and the President and the loyalty that had entrapped him into this accursed situation. If he'd known then what he knew now, he would never have involved Lucas and Roscoe and Skinner in the deception in the first place. The President could have found other ways to bring the traitors to justice. He'd turned them all into professional killers and now Sabre was sick of it.

He already knew they were on the downgrade. Those first executions had been done reluctantly, with distaste, and only done because of the President's orders. But gradually the killings had got easier until the time had come when all of them had experienced a certain excitement for the chase and the kill.

It had to stop. They were turning into predatory wolves and his heart was sick.

His resolve was clear. He had to go back alone, sort out the mess and find out what was being covered up.

Somewhere was a faceless man who had taken advantage of the President's orders. Someone was dealing behind the scenes, who now wanted those incriminating papers.

George Lucas interrupted his thoughts. 'It's no use, Sabre, if you leave without us, we're all set to follow your trail. Skinner's determined. He says we're his family and he wouldn't know how to operate if he wasn't given orders and Johnny . . . well, he's an outcast, not wanted by his tribe and certainly not by white men. He's sticking around, Sabre, so you might as well get used to the idea.'

Sabre put a hand on George's shoulder. Emotion made him grit his teeth.

'You know it will be dangerous?'

'It always has been. This time it's coming from a different quarter, that's all. We're being hunted instead of doing the hunting. It'll make a change.' He grinned to make light of it.

'Right, then we move out tomorrow and move up north. We take what rations we can carry and bypass the towns. I don't want any Pinkerton spies reporting on our whereabouts. If we can we'll go by railroad and if we can't we'll take to the mountain trails and leave the main trails behind.'

It was a long arduous journey. Sabre studied the papers in the strongbox, kept the ones which he thought would help him and jettisoned the rest with the box in a crevice in the mountains.

There was still no clue as to who the faceless man was. Sabre was reckoning on surprise when it came to a showdown. The others studiously refrained from asking about the contents of the papers. They trusted him to talk when the time was right. They all knew that the less they knew the better if there was a chance of any of them being captured by the enemy.

It was hard, gruelling going. They needed a change of horses and traded for eight fresh horses in the small town of Buffalo Creek, the small-town trader keen and eager to do business. Two horses were to be used as packhorses. Sabre paid in gold which made the ostler curious. He asked questions but Sabre was sharp and noncommittal.

They visited the town's one store and bought what they would require for a long haul. Both the storeman and the ostler watched them ride out. They'd not even stopped for a beer. Most peculiar. The storeman mentioned the strangers to the local sheriff and described the bunch of men. The sheriff looked thoughtful. There had been a telegraph message about a gang with an Indian and black man riding with them. The sheriff got excited. There was a big reward for the capture of those desperadoes.

He sent a message to Washington.

They moved on. Now they were bypassing small towns and riding the Indian trails. They had more than six hundred miles to travel and Sabre was determined to keep up the pace, then they hit the Santa Fe railroad and waited for the first train to come along.

They rested for two days before they heard the faraway warning hoot of the engine. It would stop at this small rail-stop to pick up water and to load any cattle or horses destined for the East.

Everything went smoothly. They stayed with the horses in the stock car, all relieved to ease their legs and take a rest. No one saw the tall, rangy stranger asking about them from the station-master, who could give very little information about the bunch of men. He'd assumed they were ranchers going home from a cattle-run.

The wires hummed and far away the man who took the message as Aloysius Dart, smiled and hastily sent a message to his boss. The hunters were closing in.

The train stopped at Fort Lowden, now crumbling away from disuse, but around it had grown up a thriving township. Again the engine took on water and wood and the driver and the overseer of the train visited the railway office before proceeding on their way.

Sabre watched and waited. He didn't like the stopping, especially in busy stations. Through the slats of the stock-car he could see men looking up and down the track before they came aboard. The stationmaster watched too.

It was as if they expected someone to leave the train in a hurry.

Sabre climbed to his feet.

'I don't like it. I've got a queer feelin' at the back of my neck. We'll get off when the train slows going up the next gradient.'

'You worry too much,' said George Lucas comfortably. 'Just settle down. We can move a lot faster by train than we can on horseback and we've Carla to think of.'

'Carla knows she's got to keep up, or she leaves us,' Sabre said evenly. 'I'm tellin' you, somethin' was goin' on back there. I think they're on to us.'

'Hell! How could they? We've been careful all the way. Dammit, Sabre, be reasonable!'

Sabre did not answer but stood by the slats of the stock-car gazing out at the passing scenery as the train rattled along the tracks.

Then as the train puffed past a small depot without stopping he noticed a small group of men on horseback

166

watching the train and the bow-legged stationmaster-cum-telegrapher stood at the door of his small office, watching too.

So that was it. The lines had been humming. No doubt there was an alert at every stop. The train had been ordered not to stop. The President's hunters did not want any publicity for what they were about to do . . .

Sabre spun around.

'Right, everyone! Get ready to move! Carla, get aboard your horse and wait for a signal to ride. Joshua and Johnny, be ready. Take control of the packhorses and go out in front of Carla.'

'And me, Sabre?' George asked. He was a little put out but didn't question Sabre's commands. He knew Sabre. If he smelled danger it must be all around them.

'You and me are going to roll back the shutters at the right time. There'll be no ramp, folks, and we'll be on the move. So get it right first time. And

George, keep your gun-hand ready to shoot!'

George grunted. That went without saying.

The train rattled on and the miles slipped by. Sabre wondered just how far behind the posse was. They must have calculated somewhere along the line where they would strike. Sabre had to out-think them.

Then suddenly the train faltered, the steady rhythm slowed down and Sabre's nerves tightened.

'Be ready, folks,' he called warningly.

Carla went to her horse. She stroked and calmed her, then leapt lightly aboard. Fortunately all the animals had been headed towards the opening of the double doors, where the ramp would be laid down. She loosed the bridle-rope and waited, feeling butterflies in her belly. She'd never jumped her horse from a moving train.

Johnny and Joshua unloosened their horses, reached for their packhorses' ropes and waited. It would be some feat to jump two horses together, but the packhorses always followed the riding horses so there was a good measure of success.

The train began its slow climb up the gradient. Sabre watched through the slats and judged when the time was right. He spied a clump of trees. The ground underneath was a gentle slope. It would do. The horses would get a grip . . .

'*Now!*' he yelled. He and George slid back the heavy doors. First Johnny took the plunge. The horses slid and slipped but finally found their feet Joshua followed with a yell and a kick in the ribs at the horse under him.

Sabre took a deep breath. They'd landed safely. Carla looked a little frightened. Sabre lunged forward and slapped her mare sharply on the rump. The animal took a great leap and landed nearly on her knees, but Carla pulled at her head and she staggered upright and galloped away.

Sabre grinned at George.

'You first, I'll follow fast, so keep on gallopin'.'

George did not answer but sprang up on his black's back and giving a Yankee victory shout took off with a magnificent leap into the air.

Sabre followed, and the train, with its stock-car doors left open, puffed on its way.

★　★　★

They had regrouped and all were laughing in relief that there were no casualties. They'd done something they'd never tried before and now they were ready to ride.

It was Johnny who raised the alarm. There were men coming over the horizon from in front of them and a bunch riding along the rail tracks behind them.

'The bastards thought they would catch us in a pincer movement,' Sabre said disgustedly. 'The sooner we get

170

away from here the better!'

They rode at a sharp angle away from the tracks. It would take them in a roundabout way but safer as they made their way towards Washington DC.

★   ★   ★

The two sets of riders met at the next train-stop. They surveyed the open stock-car and Nick Saunders, Pinkerton ace agent, swore mightily.

'How in hell did they know we were on their trail?' he growled, looking at the leader of the second group.

The man shrugged.

'They're a smart bunch, Nick. They're not your usual misfits. They're military men, remember.'

'Mebbe they were never on the train,' someone muttered. Nick glanced sharply at the man.

'You fool! Of course they were! The group were reported as to buyin' tickets for the whole of the run to Sante Fe, the black and the Indian with them. Of course they were on it!'

'It could have been a blind. We don't even know if they dug that there gold up.'

'They paid in gold, idiot! Where else would they get new-minted gold? Of course they were on it! We'll have to ride back along the tracks and see if we can find their tracks. There's a lot of trees near the tracks.'

'Yeh, and there's a gradient where the train slows as it climbs,' said one of the local men.

'That's it then,' said Nick Saunders. 'We'll ride back and find this place and with luck we can follow behind.'

It was a grim bunch who started back along the railtracks. It could turn out to be a hard gruelling slog, looking for Sabre Wilde and his bunch, and there would be hell to pay if they failed.

6

The President sat at the head of a small oval conference-table. He was in a raging temper and all those present cringed a little. Each and every one of them would suffer during the next hour.

'I can't understand it! I'm surrounded by incompetent fools and idiots! I order a perfectly simple operation and it can't be done! That man and his followers should have been picked up quietly and discreetly and brought back here and what happens? Someone talks and the goddamned bastards disappear!'

'It wasn't just like that, Mr President, sir.' General Fothergill courageously interrupted the angry flow. 'No one talked. He's astute. He read the signs when you gave no names to follow up. He's got the instincts of a wild animal . . . '

'He *is* a wild animal!' snarled the President. And who made him that way, thought General Fothergill as he turned a bland face to his president.

'No more than anyone would be if they were in his situation, sir.'

'Whose side are you on, Fothergill?'

'You know my answer to that, sir. No man in his right mind would expect to capture him and his men so easily.'

'Are you insinuating, General, that I'm not in my right mind?'

General Fothergill looked uncomfortable.

'Sir, that was a figure of speech, no disrespect intended.'

'I should hope not! Now let's get back to facts. The last we know about his whereabouts is that they all jumped off some goddamn train and disappeared into thin air. Right?'

There was a general nodding of heads. The boss of the Pinkerton Agency cleared his throat.

'I might say, sir, that I've put my ace agent on to the case. He's sworn to secrecy and will do everything in his power to arrest all of them quietly and bring them back to Washington.'

'With the location of the gold, I presume?'

'Sir, we have reason to believe he has already dug up his gold. Their fares on the train were paid in new-minted gold. Therefore . . . '

'Yes, yes, I understand your reasoning, Mr Pinkerton. Well, I want Horatio Wilde, dead or alive! You hear me? Dead with the proof of his death, or brought back for questioning, and I want that gold returned to the Treasury before I leave office!'

He stood up and stretched. He reminded General Fothergill of a bird of prey in his black clothes, his neck stuck forward between rounded shoulders and that cold gleam in his eyes. He moved towards the door.

'I leave you gentlemen to discuss what to do next. I have business in the Oval Office. Good day to you all.'

The men at the table all let out a sigh

of relief. It had gone more easily than they had expected. General Fothergill eyed them all thoughtfully. Now they would get down to the brass tacks of the situation.

His eyes slid easily over Mr Pinkerton. He was a newcomer to the group. He didn't matter. He looked thoughtfully at Berny Rotherheim, the Minister for Internal Financial Affairs and rested his eyes a little longer on the man's secretary, who was sitting making notes. Then his gaze went to his own liaison officer, Marcus Shane, who'd taken and relayed the messages sent to Aloysius Dart. He wondered about Marcus . . . Had his style of living changed subtly over last three years? There were rumours of gun-running activities and discrepancies in government military supplies. General Fothergill wondered uneasily if he was getting too old for his job. If he wasn't careful and there *was* something to hide, he could find himself the scapegoat. His heart quickened at the thought.

'Now, gentlemen, let's put our cards on the table. I want to know what's going on and I want to know what is in the strongbox that stirred up so much fuss. Come, gentlemen, this is no time for secrets. Major Wilde is a loose cannon until he is caught and silenced and I want to know what he knows that makes him so dangerous. One of you must know what's going on, so let's have it and then we can plan what to do!'

★   ★   ★

They'd found a perfect place to hole up and get some needed rest. They were camped on the edge of a small stream and behind was a rising butte, easily scaled, so Johnny and Joshua could take turns at guard duty. Also there were rock formations and a cave easy of access to house the horses and the packs. There was good grass beside the stream and during daylight hours the horses were tethered close by to eat their fill and rest.

They built a fire, because they were sheltered from below by a stand of trees and the fire and smoke would not be easily detected. After the evening meal they held a conference as to what Sabre aimed to do. He was adamant on going on to Washington, to the others' disapproval. They wanted for them all to make for Canada and make a new life together, only Johnny was non-committal. He would follow Sabre Wilde anywhere he wanted to go.

'I've got to face those bastards in Washington. I'm not goin' to run and hide for ever. I want the truth to come out. Someone's got to pay. The papers I hold are proof that skulduggery was goin' on under the President's nose, and I aim to bring the scandal to the public's notice. There's more to this manhunt than the fact that we didn't return that gold, or why didn't the President bring up the matter in the first instance?'

Nobody had an answer to that.

They rested for two days, Carla making the most of the time by washing clothes and bathing, and bullying the others into bathing and shaving and reminding them they weren't just animals on the run.

Johnny was on one of his early-morning sun meditations when disaster struck. Joshua was down at the stream collecting water for breakfast coffee when a bullet slammed into his back punching him high, then his body dropped into the shallow water where he lay still.

Nick Saunders grinned at the man crouching near him on the other side of the stream.

'Got the bastard! Watch for the others, men, and try and take Wilde alive!'

At once there was a stirring on the other side of the stream and two shots crashed simultaneously into the brush where Nick Saunders and two of his men lay. He heard a yelp. The bastards had been quick to spot where that first shot had come from.

Then it seemed that flame and smoke spouted from several places at once. They'd not surprised the party sleeping even though it was just before dawn.

'Spread out, boys,' Nick Saunders roared. 'The sons of bitches are well forted-up, blast them!' As he shouted a fusillade of shots crashed through the brushwood and someone cursed.

They could hear horses squealing and knew they must be in the dark cave. Well, if they couldn't see the targets they were looking for, they could blast the inside of the cave with shots and maybe kill or injure the horses.

'Fire into the cave, boys,' Nick Saunders shouted. 'Get the horses! It'll slow them down. They'll not get the chance of a getaway!'

A dozen slugs slammed into the cave. There were the sounds of horses squealing. One of Nick's men forgot caution and stood up to get a better shot. Suddenly he was slammed up against a cottontree. He slumped to the ground and lay still.

'Damn fool!' grumbled Nick Saunders. 'Watch yorselves, boys. These bastards are military-trained. They're not wasting no ammo. They're makin' every shot count!'

But now the shots were coming from overhead thick and fast and in volleys. It looked as if Sabre had his few followers working to a pattern, military style.

Nick Saunders set his teeth. It hadn't been such a surprise as he'd intended.

Then a surprise shot came from far up above and Nick spied the Indian just crouching behind a boulder. He waited, but was fooled. The wily Indian had rolled away and came up for another snap shot feet from where he had been seen. Nick Saunders ground his teeth in frustration. Meanwhile shots were traded on both sides.

Then Sabre heard stones rattling from above and guessed Johnny was about to join them. He took a chance and dived behind another rock. Carla yelled and made to stop him. For a moment she was exposed and a bullet exploded beside her as George Lucas roughly pulled her back.

'Fool!' he shouted angrily. 'What in hell d'you think you're doing?'

'Sabre,' she gasped, 'I thought — '

'Stop thinking, and keep your mind on those bastards out there!' His face was white and for a moment he hated her for causing him such pain. Then he forced himself to put all thoughts of her from him and carry on watching out for the enemy.

Carla crawled away from him and took refuge behind another boulder. There was tumult in her heart, hate for George for stopping her from following Sabre, hate for Sabre for not wanting her, all mixed up with the hate that encompassed the whole world. She was in a killing mood. She hated twice over the men surrounding them. She ground her teeth in an upsurge of that hatred.

Coldly she drew a bead on an incautious head that peeped from the foliage below. She exulted at the scream and the glimpse of red as the head disappeared into the brush. Another one down!

She fought like a tigress and gloried in it.

Johnny joined Sabre behind his boulder. He was panting a little with the effort of scrambling on his belly.

'There's up to two hands out there.' He raised all his fingers.

'Ten?' Sabre acknowledged. 'Those two bunches got together then. At least we know there's no more to come. Where's Skinner? Have you seen him?'

Johnny nodded upwards.

'He's movin', military style. Shoot and roll.'

'Good.'

Sabre took aim and fired across the stream from where seconds before had come a puff of smoke. He wished the bastards would come out in the open. They were wasting bullets, but sometimes there was the scream of a man and he knew that not every shot was wasted.

How many times had he hit the target? Three? Four? The men out there must be getting more sparse on the ground. Vaguely he heard the rifle-fire of the others, always in military fashion. He was proud of them. Even Carla was keeping a cool head.

He didn't know of the little drama between George and Carla and would have dismissed it if he had known. His only thought now was to save himself and the others and God damn the rest.

Two hours later, when the sun was beginning to make itself felt, there was a lull. A stentorian voice bellowed forth from down below.

'Major Wilde? Can you hear me? I want you to surrender your arms and come out with your hands up. You're surrounded, Major. You can't win this battle, Major.'

'Go to hell, whoever you are!' bawled Sabre. 'As for surroundin' us, fat chance! You've lost more than half yor men. Go back to Washington and tell those bastards there that I'll be back when I'm good and ready. Got that?'

'I've got my orders, Major. I've got to take you back!'

'Then come and get me, if you can!' Sabre pumped a couple of bullets in the direction of the voice. There was a scream and everything went quiet. Sabre sighed. Perhaps a death, or an injured man. In either case he was getting mighty sick of this senseless violence.

The silence continued and Skinner up above got impatient and slithered down to join Sabre and Johnny. 'What's it mean, sir? Have they given up?'

'No. Probably arguin' who's in charge. I've a feelin' I got the boss feller,' Sabre said musingly, his eyes still roving over the brush on the other side of the stream.

Johnny took off his army hat, put it on his rifle barrel and held it up. He moved along the boulder holding it head high. No shots came. They waited.

Then George Lucas's voice came to them.

'I think the sons of bitches have moved out, Sabre. I think I'll take a look-see.'

'Watch yorself, George. It could be a trap.'

But it wasn't. Johnny followed George, who backtracked along the stream and found the place where their horses had been tethered and then untied in a hurry as the remainder of the bunch retreated. It looked as if both leaders had been killed and the survivors, reckoning it was none of their business, had made tracks.

It was when they were finding and counting the dead that the tragedy happened. Sabre was turning a body over to check it out when an apparently lifeless man lifted himself and grunted, waving an unsteady Colt at Sabre's back. Carla saw the movement and rushed at Sabre to knock him out of the way. She took the bullet meant for Sabre in the back. The impact flung her into the air and as she came down a crimson patch appeared on her shirt.

She sprawled at Sabre's feet, quite dead.

A murderous rage filled Sabre. He pumped shot after shot into the dying man and then kicked his head.

'God damn you, you son of a bitch!' Then he knelt down beside Carla and turned her gently over. But there was no breath in her, her eyes were closed. It was as if she was asleep. He sighed, as George Lucas came running up.

'What happened, Sabre? I heard shots.' He cast his eyes down at Carla, stunned, appalled. He shook his head as if he couldn't believe his eyes.

Sabre looked up at him without speaking but glanced at the bullet-ridden man and George understood. He pushed Sabre away. 'I'll deal with her. Leave her to me.' He scooped her up and took her away. Sabre gestured to Skinner and Johnny to leave them alone.

It was a subdued party who went into the cave to survey the horses. There were two left standing: the packhorses that had been tethered furthest from the entrance. One had been grazed on the rump but apart from the trembling they were in good shape.

They repacked the gold on to the two animals. They would walk until they could find other horses. Each man carried a share of the remaining food and a canteen of water. All were silent as they left that place for the last time.

Each one had visited the graves of Joshua and Carla lying side by side with small rough crosses at their heads to mark their passing. Each wrestled with sombre thoughts but all had one thing in common. They wanted vengeance on those who'd ordered their deaths.

$\star$ $\star$ $\star$

Back in Washington, the boss of the Pinkerton Agency was growing uneasy. It had been days since his best man Nick Saunders had set forth on this delicate mission. He should at least have wired at given intervals his report on progress. Of course, working on a case out West wasn't like operating back East. There weren't the facilities for one thing. He could only wait.

But there was continual pressure from those big nobs in Washington who had no idea what was entailed when they set orders in motion. That pressure was getting between him and his victuals besides giving him severe headaches.

He paced his office continually, snapped at his clerks and made life hell for everyone, even his wife.

The day came when he had to face the President and the small group of men who sat with accusing faces waiting for his results. He shook his head.

'I'm sorry, Mr President and gentlemen, I'm afraid I have nothing to report. My best man has let me down . . .'

'You mean that damned major is still on the loose?' barked the President. Allan Pinkerton bowed his head.

'Sir, I know not. He could be on the loose, as you say, or else he could be dead. I do not know.'

The President rapped the table with a bony fist.

'God dammit, Pinkerton, your agency has been puffed up out of all proportion! Your men are no better than any of the marshals out there. I could have hired men at half the price and come up with what you've come up with!'

Allan Pinkerton cringed. 'Sir, that's not fair on my men! These were special circumstances. Secrecy made it harder. We didn't have the usual help or — '

'Enough! What do we do now?' The President looked around at his close associates who were all looking glum and worried. 'I take it that we can assume that Major Horatio Wilde is loose out there and plotting God knows what!'

The men looked at each other. Major Wilde was no fool. He would have assessed the situation.

Berny Rotherheim looked around at

his associates and especially meaning-fully at his secretary and Marcus Shane. Then he coughed.

'Mr President, sir, about that gold . . . '

'Yes, yes, Bernie, what about it?' Johnson asked sharply.

'I could arrange a . . . er . . . bill of sale, as it were to cover . . . '

'You mean cook the books?'

All the men present sat back in their chairs, gasping inwardly at the President's bluntness.

'I wouldn't go so far as to describe it in those terms, sir,' Berny Rotherheim said with an oily grin which he wiped from his face at the President's next words.

'Damn it, Berny, what else would you call it? You're good at accounts and other things, I take it. There's other things to consider. Those papers for one.'

'Sir, I don't know who was respon-sible for leaving that strongbox aboard that train when it was cleared for that . . . er . . . special operation, but whoever he was, he should be shot!'

There were murmurs of hear, hear!

'Well, the mistake was made and we'll have to live with it but this business with Wilde must be resolved, gentlemen. Mr Pinkerton, we'll give you another chance, otherwise we'll have to hire ourselves a real professional killer. Understand me, Mr Pinkerton?'

'Yes, sir, absolutely, sir.'

The President rose to indicate the end of the meeting.

'I don't want to see you again until you bring me Wilde, or proof of his death. Good morning, gentlemen!'

★ ★ ★

Sabre sat opposite George Lucas and Ned Skinner with the flickering fire between them. It was at these times at night, when they ate their scratch meals that they missed Carla and Joshua. George, who was morose and withdrawn these days, suffered most.

Johnny Eagle Eye, always the loner, missed Joshua and during the hours when he remained apart from the others included Joshua in his prayers for his dead ancestors.

Now, having eaten, he was perched up in the shelter of an overhanging rock, watching the trail ahead of and behind them as he sat cross-legged, meditating. He could see the fire flickering below and the three dark shapes clustered around it. Part of him was alert, the other part of him seeking out memories both sad and happy.

Below, the men talked softly.

'What do we know of Marcus Shane?' Sabre asked. George Lucas shrugged his shoulders.

'He's civilian, works with General Fothergill and is trusted by him, hence the knowing of the code, Aloysius Dart. Has got a small ranch outside Washington but spends most of his time in Washington.'

Ned Skinner looked from one to the other.

'I remember when I was in Washington acting as your batman, sir, seeing him with that secretary of that creep, Rotherheim. I think his name was Dwight Bannerman.'

'Bannerman, eh?' Sabre rubbed at his bristly chin. It itched now that the hair was growing back. 'You think they could all be in this thing together?' He looked at George Lucas.

George lifted his shoulders and grimaced a little.

'Smells fishy. Looks to me like Rotherheim has it all sewed up with both Shane and Bannerman there, to make things easy. Bannerman's his secretary and Shane works for the general, so what better set-up could you have?'

'So between them all they have access to government and military equipment and stores?' Wilde nodded thoughtfully. 'And dealing with genuine suppliers and syphonin' off part of consignments with false bills of sale, hence the gun-running.'

'Those papers in the box showed details and accounting of where the stores were being shipped. I suppose it's possible to backtrack and get back to the suppliers. My father is implicated in those papers,' George said quietly 'Obviously one of his managers has been got at. He needs to know.'

'What about the general? Is he in with them, and what about the President himself?'

'Ah, the President. I don't think he'd stoop to financial fraud. I think he's interested only in covering his tracks with you. The bastard wants to leave office with a clean slate and smelling of roses!'

'So. I think we should pay the general a visit and find out which side he's on. But first we bury the gold and I know just the place.'

The gold having been duly buried in the heart of the Shenandoah Hills the four men rode away, all wondering whether they would be alive to come back and claim those bags.

They rode across country, stopping only to eat and rest the horses. They were all used to long forced marches with the military so it was no real hardship. Their goal now was to confront General Fothergill and find out the truth.

★ ★ ★

The boss of the Pinkerton Agency was frustrated and ill-tempered. He snapped at his Number One, the man he most trusted for these illicit affairs. Damn the President and his all-powering need for secrecy. This undercover work made it hard to get information which he sadly needed. The old fool didn't understand that detective work meant using the telegraph and all the contacts he had in other states. They were working blind like goddamn piddling marshals in their own backyards.

He was ranting and raving to his Number One who waited patiently to get a word in. He sighed as he waited. Then when the boss drew breath he said quietly,

'What about General Fothergill?'

'Goddamn it, what about him?'

'Well, the major trusts him. Couldn't we put a man on him? Maybe the major might come to see him.'

Allan Pinkerton stopped in his tracks. Why hadn't he thought of that? For a moment he considered, then he turned swiftly.

'Ah, yes, I thought of that. In fact I was about to give orders . . . ' His mind was clocking the possibilities. He didn't see the smile on his man's face, and he certainly didn't know what was passing through his mind.

'Yes, I've got some figuring to do. We'll put a man on to watch him. It should be easy. I understand he's not in good odour with the President and has retired to his country ranch.'

★   ★   ★

General Fothergill leaned back in his chair, a half-empty wineglass held loosely in his hand. It had been a good dinner. He glanced at his secretary, Marcus Shane, and then at his visitors. All seemed replete. He frowned a little. He didn't like Berny Rotherheim, never had, and he often wondered why the President put so much faith in him. He certainly didn't like his unctuous dogsbody, the so-called secretary, Dwight Bannerman, who put him in mind of a smooth gambler rather than a clerk in an office. He noticed the bulge under his left arm. The bastard hadn't even the courtesy to come to the dinner table unarmed.

'Well, gentlemen, shall we now adjourn to my study and talk business?' The general looked meaningly at his housekeeper, who was busy at the sideboard putting brandy glasses on a tray along with the decanter. 'Hannah, we'll take brandy and coffee in my study.'

They settled in the book-lined room

on comfortable leather chairs. General Fothergill's genial host's face now turned grim.

'Now gentlemen, please explain your business. There is no one to overhear what you say, so you can be quite frank.'

★　★　★

It was nearly midnight and the four riders could see the dim light still burning in the ranch house. Sabre Wilde put up a hand and they drew rein. They looked down the hillside to the buildings below. All was quiet. They could hear horses in the corral behind the main house. A lowing of cattle came from the far hillside. It was a typical night when all lights should have been out and the inmates should have been sleeping.

But that one light disturbed Sabre Wilde. He had the instincts of a prowling cat. He knew from old that the old man retired early. He'd said it many times in his hearing that he liked his bed, even when on campaigns. So why was he now burning the midnight oil?

Voices carried on the cold night air. He spoke softly.

'We'll tether the horses in that stand of trees.' He indicated some trees in a cluster overlooking the corral, 'and then we'll spread out. You'll take the back, George, and Ned, you check the bunk-house and I'll take the front. I want to have a look in that lighted window. Come runnin' if there's trouble. You, Johnny, get yourself squatting on that knoll yonder and keep a look-out. If anything stirs give us the old owlhoot call.'

Johnny nodded. He and his horse turned and made for the rising ground not far from the house where he could watch and wait.

Horses tethered, the three men moved like shadows, disappearing into the night. In the distance, a coyote howled for his mate but around the ranch all was quiet.

Sabre frowned when he saw the surrey tucked away under a giant shade-tree with the horses still in the shafts. So, General Fothergill had company. He ran across the yard, doubled over for fear curious eyes were looking out of a darkened window. He waited but all was quiet.

He tiptoed on to the veranda and made his way along to the lighted window. He could see General Fothergill sitting close to a nearly extinct fire. He looked worried, not like a man entertaining friends. He looked decidedly edgy.

He saw the silhouettes of two men with their backs to the window but couldn't identify them. A third man he could see but only his crossed legs. It looked as if he was sitting at ease.

He strained to listen but could only hear the muffled sounds of voices. The general seemed to be speaking forcefully. Then the man with crossed legs stood up. Sabre drew a deep breath as Berny Rotherheim stood over the general and pointed his finger at him in a threatening manner.

So, he could almost guarantee that the other two men were Shane and Bannerman. Sabre smiled. It couldn't have been better. He waited. George Lucas and Skinner would be reporting back any time now. He tested with probing fingers the frame of the window. The wood was old and half rotten.

He turned when he sensed rather than heard the movements behind him. Both Lucas and Skinner were there, their eyes gleaming in anticipation.

'Look in there,' he whispered. Both men took a swift glance. Then Sabre gestured to the window. Two of them could burst through it together. Both men nodded. They understood.

'Now!'

Lucas and Skinner leapt forward, shoulders braced as the frame burst inwards, showering glass everywhere.

General Fothergill was in shock as were the three men who'd spun around, mouths agape, feeling blindly for guns they couldn't grasp.

Then Sabre Wilde calmly stepped through the ruined window, a Colt .45 in each hand.

'Well, well, General and gentlemen, so we meet again. So accommodating of you all to be together. It saves me and my colleagues from hunting you up separately!'

He smiled grimly at them all, his teeth showing sharply in his dark face. He looked fierce with his shaggy newly grown hair on his head, the red cicatrix running down his cheek making him look like the devil himself.

Berny Rotherheim looked at him with horror. He wasn't a fighting man. He was better at plotting and planning and leaving the dirty work to others. His bowels turned to water.

'Major Wilde, there's been some mistake . . . ' he began in a choked voice. 'I had no hand in ordering you to be shot! I'm only interested in getting the gold back for the Treasury. General Fothergill will bear me out. It was all the President's doing! I had nothing to do with it, believe me!' He was babbling and tiny globules of spit were running down one side of his mouth.

He wanted to be sick and the pain in his guts was doubling him over. The look in the major's eyes as they bored into him was conjuring up the horrors of hell for him.

Sabre cocked his right-hand pistol. It was pointed at Rotherheim's chest.

'Keep on talkin', mister. I want to know everything.'

'Everything? What do you mean?'

'I mean all about your arrangements with these two crooks here. I know all about their gun-running activities. General, were you feathering your nest too?' For the first time, Sabre looked directly at his old commanding officer.

The old man shook his head and looked down at his hands which were twitching in his lap. It was as if he couldn't control himself.

'No, I swear it, Major. All I did was obey orders. I never approved of you and your men sacrificing yourselves, but a dirty job had to be done. There were many traitors who deserved to die, but I never agreed with the President that you should be hounded down for what you did. As for the other business, I didn't know the Treasury was being fleeced. God knows what will happen if this scandal gets out!'

'You needn't worry, General. You forget, I'm a professional killer with years of experience. We'll take these crooks off your hands and dispose of them. It'll be a nine days' wonder but when the new elections get under way, folks in Washington will forget all about them!'

'Hey! What d'you mean, dispose of us?' Dwight Bannerman found his voice and despite being covered by George Lucas, went for the gun in his shoulder holster.

There was an explosion which deafened the eardrums. Bannerman seemed to leap in the air, then he hit the wall with some force. He sagged to the ground, a red bloody smear running down the wall. He was quite dead. George Lucas shrugged, holding the smoking gun.

'Sorry, Sabre, but it had to be done.'

'Yes, well no harm done. Everything seems quiet outside.'

But that shot had been heard by the Pinkerton man who was supposed to be on duty, watching for any suspicious arrivals.

He'd missed seeing the three shadowy figures making for the ranch house, because he was bored and resentful that he had to be on guard when his buddies were hunkered down in the valley below along with the boss all cosylike. So he'd had a nip or three from his hip-flask and had risked making himself a cigarette and smoking it in the shadow of a rock. Now the shot galvanized him into action.

What in hell . . . ? Goddamnit! If some bastard had got in there without him reporting it he'd be for the high jump!

He fired his rifle into the air and took a mighty leap down from the hummock from where he was supposed to be watching. The four men with Allan Pinkerton rolled out of their blankets, cursing under their breath but ready for action.

As he scrambled to his feet, the look-out man sensed a movement behind him. He twisted round and stared the Apache in the face. Shock paralysed him, and he could only watch as the raised hand with the knife glinting in the moonlight came down and bit deeply into his chest. He died without a sound.

Inside the ranch house, Marcus Shane stared unbelievingly at the crumpled figure on the floor. Then panic siezed him. As the smoke cleared he took a flying leap for the broken window, plunged through it and landed on his knees.

Sabre's gun roared but it was reflex action and the bullet ploughed into the wall. George Lucas and young Ned both got to the window together; there was a delay before both hit the ground. Sabre fumed because they were in the line of fire.

But it was too late for a snap shot at the fleeing man. He'd taken advantage of the shadows.

'Spread out, fellers,' bawled Sabre. 'He'll want a horse!' Already there was the sound of horses snorting, disturbed from their rest.

Then came the rifle-fire. Sabre ducked as the lead shot whistled past him. It came from the surrey. At the same moment the surrey moved with a jerk as the two horses pulling it set off at a gallop at the crack of a whip. The bulk of the vehicle hid Shane and Sabre cursed, but sent a couple of shots hoping to cripple one of the horses.

Then, as the surrey rocked and swayed on the narrow trail leading into town, he saw the shadow of a figure plummeting down from the rocks above. It landed with a crash on the canopy of the buggy.

Sabre watched while Shane and Johnny became a mass of struggling arms and legs. He turned back to the house when he saw the body of Shane hit the ground. Johnny followed him as the two horses panicked and galloped off, the surrey swaying and eventually turning over as the horses squealed and kicked before coming to rest with their heads down.

In the ranch house Ned Skinner stood over Berny Rotherheim who was now crouching on the floor, blood pouring out from his nose. General Fothergill was interrogating him. He looked up as Sabre joined them.

'Got the varmint?'

Sabre nodded.

'Johnny's mopping him up. What about him?' he indicated Rotherheim.

General Forthergill spoke bitterly. 'He's spewed his guts. Names, dates, the lot! He kept the President sweet by juggling the books and promising him great savings. The old man never realized he was being duped! This crook held the threat of exposure over him. He knew from the beginning what the President ordered you to do and used it as a lever. I had no inkling. I thought our arrangement with you was just between us three and the men you chose for their loyalty to you. I'm sorry, Major. We botched it. It will hurt the Democrats if all this is made public. The Republicans will be hanging out the bunting.'

Sabre gave a wry smile.

'As far as I and my men are concerned, the damage to us is done. It can't be changed. We can only go on to make new lives.'

'What about him?'

Sabre looked thoughtfully at the cowering man who was listening avidly to what the general was reporting. He saw the message in Sabre's eyes.

'For God's sake! I promise I'll never speak of these matters! I'll resign on the grounds of ill-health. If the Republicans win the election I'll be out anyway! I'll be as silent as the grave, I promise you!'

Sabre leaned forward and lifted Rotherheim's chin high with the muzzle of his Colt.45.

'Have you forgotten something?'

The man's eyes flickered.

'What have I forgotten? For God's sake, have mercy! I've got a wife and kids!'

'You and that carrion you run with kept the war going longer than it should have done. You keep it going now with the guns you've been selling in Mexico and to the Indians. You've cost lives, Rotherheim.'

'Look, I'm not responsible for what happened to the supplies and guns after they left Washington! That was up to others!'

Sabre laughed harshly.

'Who supplied the names to the President for me to dispatch eh? How many of those men were executed for your benefit? How many men did we kill for you, Mr Rotherheim?'

'I swear they were all approved by the President!'

Rotherheim's forehead dripped with

sweat. His face twisted and suddenly he was crying. A stench filled the air as his bowels erupted. General Fothergill turned away, sick to his stomach. He saw by the look on Sabre's face that they had done their job too well. Sabre Wilde had passed over the line between being a soldier and a cold killing-machine. He was enjoying the terror that he was evoking in this man.

'For the love of God, Major, have done . . . ' Fothergill beseeched. 'Stop this playing cat and mouse . . . '

Slowly Sabre raised the Colt in his right hand and pointed it at Rother-heim's head.

'You're right, General. One should never hesitate when killing a rat!' He pulled the trigger, and Rotherheim slumped to the floor, quite dead.

That shot triggered a thundering of hoofs from outside. George Lucas, who'd remained silent and passive, leapt to the window. He cursed at what he saw.

The false dawn was breaking and he

could see the bunch of riders sweeping down the track. They were shooting as they came.

'Here comes the cavalry,' George exclaimed, 'and they mean business.' He snatched up the general's rifle and sent a shot amongst the riders. They immediately fanned out, shooting as they came.

'So the President's getting his way after all.' Sabre laughed wildly. 'Well, if they want me they'll have to smoke us out first!'

Ned Skinner checked the windows of the rest of the ranch house while General Fothergill quickly opened the glass-fronted case where he kept his army rifles and ammunition. He threw a rifle to each of them and hefted a shotgun himself.

Sabre eyed him curiously.

'You'd fire at Pinkerton's men? You'd be going against the President's orders!'

'To hell with orders! I know what's right and what's wrong. If justice was done, you'd be riding away from here and making a new life for yourselves. I'm going to help you do just that.'

'I'm mighty pleased and touched, General. I'll not forget that!'

Then they both turned to the business at hand. As the dawn broke and the first rays of the sun came over the horizon, the battle began.

At first both sides were wary and conserving bullets. The housekeeper who slept in a back room came screaming into the hall and was told sharply to get back to her room and keep away from her window.

Allan Pinkerton was nonplussed. The damned ranch was like a fortress with shutters at the windows. Only the one window was smashed and vulnerable and that was where most of the firing was coming from. He tried a new tack.

Standing well back out of range he bawled his ultimatum.

'General Fothergill, we know you're harbouring the man the President wants, and his men. Do you want to see your home burned to the ground and yourself regarded as a traitor? If you don't, send Sabre Wilde out to me and nothing will be said about this affair.'

'Go to hell!' the stentorian voice of General Fothergill answered back.

Allan Pinkerton wasn't used to wild Western ways. He was from back East and now he was angry at his dilemma. He should have had a posse of local men with him but his hands had been tied because of the need for secrecy. He cursed the President under his breath. He tried persuasion on the major.

'Major Wilde, all we want to do is take you back for the President to interview you. This matter of the gold and your breach of duty is most important. Surrendering to me would save a lot of bloodshed.'

'Like the general says, go to hell! Your promises mean nothing. You want my blood, so come and get me if you can!'

'Right, you sonofabitch,' Allan Pinkerton said softly between gritted teeth. 'We'll do just that.'

There was a fusillade of shots and

one of Pinkerton's men yelped. Now the firing was coming from every front window and at intervals there was the sound of a powerful shotgun raking the front of the yard.

Allan Pinkerton motioned to one of his men.

'See if you can find any firebrands in that big barn yonder. We'll fire the roof.'

The man nodded and loped off. There might also be kegs of kerosene stored in one of the sheds. But he never made it. A dark shadow landed on him as he opened the creaking barn door and Johnny's knife slid between his ribs.

George Lucas spied a man climbing on the cook-house roof. He turned his smoking Colt on to him and had the satisfaction of seeing the body plummet to the ground. He gave a victory war whoop and turned once again to face the front of the house. Allan Pinkerton's bullet caught him in the throat. His eyes widened in astonishment as he choked and slid to the ground.

Sabre saw him fall from the corner of

his eye as he drew a bead on the crouching figure hiding behind a water-butt.

Sorrow and anger made him rise. It was General Fothergill who restrained him from going out there with all guns blazing.

The housekeeper's shriek startled them all.

'What in hell . . . ?' Sabre jumped into the passageway and cursed. While they'd been kept occupied at the front, the attackers had breached one of the back windows and now a grinning Pinkerton man was using the old woman as a cover for himself.

'Move a muscle, and I'll kill her!' The man brandished the gun in front of them all.

'If you do,' Sabre answered calmly, 'you're dead meat. Do you want that?'

The man's eyes flickered as Sabre went on reasonably,

'This isn't your show, mister. Why stick your neck out for Pinkerton?'

The man's hand wavered and Sabre

chose that moment to pounce. The man's hand instinctively tightened on the trigger. Ned Skinner sprang forward, and knocked Sabre out of the way and took the bullet in the chest. With a groan, he cannoned into the general who caught him as he fell.

The housekeeper screamed again. Her elbow caught her captor in the crotch. As he bent forward, Sabre's bullet tore into his head.

Suddenly there was silence in the passageway except for the woman's muffled sobs.

Then from outside came the long-drawn-out Apache yell of triumph of a brave who'd counted coup.

Sabre staggered to the front door and opened it. Johnny Eagle Eye wouldn't have given that yell unless all was clear.

He found Johnny standing over Allan Pinkerton. A dirty rag gagged his mouth and a rawhide rope was fastened around his ankles. Sabre stood with his feet apart on the verandah steps. 'It's all over then, Johnny?'

'Yes, he's the last man. I don't know what you want to do with him, boss. You decide.'

Sabre Wilde looked thoughtfully down at the boss of the Pinkerton Agency.

'You should have stuck to your own stamping-ground, mister. We do things differently out here in the West.'

'Cut the bullshit! What are you going to do with me? You're all animal, Major Wilde, and what they say about you is true!'

'What do they say about me?'

'That Major Wilde is dead and a thing with no heart and no emotions walks in your body. I pity you, Major Wilde.'

The two men glared at each other.

'Whatever I am, I have become because I was a loyal soldier and obeyed orders. Remember that when you report to the President.'

'You mean to let me go?'

Sabre shrugged.

'I don't blame you for coming after me. After all, we both obeyed orders.' He turned to Johnny who was waiting.

'Sling him over his horse. Tie him well and the horse will take him back to where he came from.'

'But, boss, is that wise?'

'We'll be long gone before he makes his report.' He turned round to General Fothergill. 'Could you persuade yor housekeeper to brew us some coffee and fix us some breakfast? We have a long way to go.'

'Of course.' The old general turned away. Then paused.

'What about the gold?'

Sabre laughed.

'What about it? That is for Johnny and me to decide.' His face turned grave and his eyes showed their hurt.

General Fothergill knew that they were wrong. Sabre Wilde, the outlaw, had heart and emotions just as the old Major Wilde had had, but now he could control them better. He called for coffee and breakfast.

They had a long way to go.

We do hope that you have enjoyed reading this large print book.

Did you know that all of our titles are available for purchase?

We publish a wide range of high quality large print books including:
Romances, Mysteries, Classics
General Fiction
Non Fiction and Westerns

Special interest titles available in large print are:
The Little Oxford Dictionary
Music Book, Song Book
Hymn Book, Service Book

Also available from us courtesy of Oxford University Press:
Young Readers' Dictionary
(large print edition)
Young Readers' Thesaurus
(large print edition)

For further information or a free brochure, please contact us at:
Ulverscroft Large Print Books Ltd.,
The Green, Bradgate Road, Anstey,
Leicester, LE7 7FU, England.
Tel: (00 44) **0116 236 4325**
Fax: (00 44) **0116 234 0205**

A TOWN CALLED TROUBLESOME

John Dyson

Matt Matthews had carved his ranch out of the wild Wyoming frontier. But he had his troubles. The big blow of '86 was catastrophic, with dead beeves littering the plains, and the oncoming winter presaged worse. On top of this, a gang of desperadoes had moved into the Snake River valley, killing, raping and rustling. All Matt can do is to take on the killers single-handed. But will he escape the hail of lead?

CABEL

Paul K. McAfee

Josh Cabel returned home from the Civil War to find his family all murdered by rioting members of Quantrill's band. The hunt for the killers led Josh to Colorado City where, after months of searching, he finally settled down to work on a ranch nearby. He saved the life of an Indian, who led him to a cache of weapons waiting for Sitting Bull's attack on the Whites. His involvement threw Cabel into grave danger. When the final confrontation came, who had the fastest — and deadlier — draw?

RIVERBOAT

Alan C. Porter

When Rufus Blake died he was found to be carrying a gold bar from a Confederate gold shipment that had disappeared twenty years before. This inspires Wes Hardiman and Ben Travis to swap horse and trail for a riverboat, the *River Queen*, on the Mississippi, in an effort to find the missing gold. Cord Duval is set on destroying the *River Queen* and he has the power and the gunmen to do it. Guns blaze as Hardiman and Travis attempt to unravel the mystery and stay alive.

McKINNEY'S LAW

Mike Stotter

McKinney didn't count on coming across a dead body in the middle of Texas. He was about to become involved in an ever-deepening mystery. The renegade Comanche warrior, Black Eagle, was on the loose, creating havoc; he didn't appear in McKinney's plans at all, not until the Comanche forced himself into his life. The US Army gave McKinney some relief to his problems, but it also added to them, and with two old friends McKinney set about bringing justice through his own law.

BLACK RIVER

Adam Wright

John Dyer has come to the insignificant little town of Black River to destroy the last living reminder of his dark past. He has come to kill. Jack Hart is determined to stop him. Only he knows the terrible truth that has driven Dyer here, and he knows that only he can beat Dyer in a gunfight. Ex-lawman Brad Harris is after Dyer too — to avenge his family. The stage is set for madness, death and vengeance.